THE MIRACLE OF CHRISTMAS

From the very beginning, miracles were always a part of Christmas. The birth of the "Son of God" was predicted by both prophets, who said He would be born of a virgin in the little city of Bethlehem, and angels, who predicted He "would save His people from their sins." His birth was announced by a heavenly chorus of angels who sang "Glory to God in the highest and on earth, peace and goodwill toward men." In addition, His birth was attended by "His Star" that supernaturally guided the "three wise men from the east" to the place where He lived so they could "worship Him."

As miraculous as was His birth, His life was even more so. In only three short years, He influenced this world for good, more than anyone who has ever lived. His teachings of love, morality, and personal concern for others were unsurpassed. Many have noted that more hospitals, schools, orphanages, churches, and humanitarian efforts to help people have been launched by his followers than before or after him. All the Greek philosophers together have not helped humanity as much as the "one Solitary life" of the "man from Nazareth." The many miracles He performed of healing blind eyes or deaf ears, twisted limbs from birth, and all manner of other diseases put Him in a category all by Himself. Only of Jesus could it be said, "He looked with compassion on the multitudes and He healed them all."

Gift giving in celebration of our Savior's birth has been enjoyed for two thousand years by the Christian world and even others who share our Christmas custom. The miracle of gift giving lives on. And, no wonder, because it was started by God Himself when "He gave us His only Son that we might have everlasting life." It was continued when His Son gave up His exalted status in heaven to become the sacrifice for our sins. Mary gave her body to God so she could birth the Christ child, and Joseph, his bride-to-be, to serve the Lord. The wise men continued that gift giving custom when they presented the Christ Child with gifts of gold, frankincense, and myrrh and that practice of giving continues even to this day. For we have all found the miracle of Jesus' teaching is true, "It is more blessed to give than to receive." Who has not been enriched by bringing joy and pleasure to someone we love at Christmastime when we give a gift that has cost us something special. I well remember the joy I received as a teenage newspaper boy in watching my single mother with three children to raise open her Christmas gift of a new Study Bible that she wanted desperately but couldn't afford. My real blessing came many years later while sorting through her effects upon her death. I turned to the front of her well-worn and much-marked Bible and read, "A love gift from my son, Tim." No doubt you have given gifts like that. Giving is its own reward.

The miracle of Christmas does not stop there. Every year at this time many who have neglected God, or ignored him much of their lives have heard a refrain in a Christmas carol, or a bible verse, or a message in a card from a friend or loved one, a children's play at church or a concert that musically gives the Christian message of faith and renewal are reminded that God loves them and wants them, like the wise men of old, to come and worship Him. Some, like the prodigal son Jesus told about, repent of their sins, return to the Father's house, and find that warm personal relationship with God they always wanted. Salvation is not something you deserve or work for, it is a miraculous gift that God alone can give and all you can do is, by faith, accept it.

It is Greg Dinallo's and my prayer that as you read this delightful book, it will not only thrill and inspire you but help you to experience the true miracle of Christmas. A personal relationship with God will enrich the rest of your life through His son who "loves you and gave Himself for you".

THE BEST CHRISTMAS GIFT

Tim LaHaye

and Gregory S. Dinallo

KENSINGTON BOOKS
http://www.kensingtonbooks.com

KENSINGTON BOOKS are published by

Kensington Publishing Corp.
850 Third Avenue
New York, NY 10022

All Kensington titles, imprints and distributed lines are available at special quantity discounts for bulk purchases for sales promotion, premiums, fund-raising, educational or institutional use.

Special book excerpts or customized printings can also be created to fit specific needs. For details, write or phone the office of the Kensington Special Sales Manager: Kensington Publishing Corp., 850 Third Avenue, New York, NY 10022. Attn. Special Sales Department. Phone: 1-800-221-2647.

Kensington and the K logo Reg. U.S. Pat. & TM Off.

Library of Congress Card Catalogue Number: 2004113882
ISBN 0-7582-1098-1

First Printing: October 2005
10 9 8 7 6 5 4 3 2 1

Printed in the United States of America

PART ONE

God rest ye merry gentlemen,
Let nothing you dismay . . .

Chapter One

The air inside the rambling cottage was alive with the chemical scent that always started Cooper's day. The fumes permeated his cupboards and clothing, and overpowered the bracing rush of brine that rode the wind to the foothills.

Cooper sat on the edge of the bed and inhaled deeply several times. The acrid bouquet was far more intoxicating than any woman's perfume or the nostalgic fragrance of heather that drifted across the highlands of his native Scotland. Even the aroma of black coffee, or whiskey for that matter, couldn't compete with it for his affection. He slipped his suspenders up over his thick shoulders, then trudged to the window and listened intently. Not for the sound of birds or surf or wind rustling the autumnal wilderness, but for the clatter of an internal combustion engine.

He always heard the truck before he could see it, snaking along the shoreline, then up a secondary road to a row of mailboxes that leaned this way and that on their angled posts. Every morning for a week, Cooper had gone out to meet it; and every morning the mud-spattered truck with RFD on the side continued past. The day Cooper decided to forego the trek, it chugged up the hill, announcing its arrival with a horn that had the honk of an angry grouse.

Cooper hurried from the cottage, his breath coming in gray puffs that hung in the frosty air, and pushed through a gate with hinges that creaked louder than his own. Underwear the color of oatmeal filled the neck of his Pendleton; and his corduroy trousers whisked with each stride, the frayed cuffs skimming brown high-top shoes that hadn't seen polish since the day they left the factory. A fibrous individual with a tanned, deeply-lined face capped by a tousled white mane, he spoke with a soft burr that sharpened when he became excited or angered, or wanted to sound charming. "How are you, Ben?"

"Fine, Mister Cooper. Just fine."

"Does that racket you're making mean you finally have my parcel?"

Ben shrugged, feigning uncertainty. "Well, when I didn't see you out here waiting, I figured maybe I'd just keep on going, but I had a change of heart."

"Real thoughtful of you, Ben."

The mailman grinned, then leaned into the back of the truck and fetched a package. It measured about ten-by-twelve-by-four inches, and was wrapped in brown paper secured with sturdy twine. "This the one?"

Cooper's wintry eyes sparkled at the sight of the postmark that identified it as *the* package. "Aye. Rochester, New York. That's my parcel. Puts me back in business. Well, I best be—"

"Good place to be these days," Ben interrupted.

Cooper nodded in tight-lipped agreement. "Not the best of times. Well, I best be—"

"Nope," Ben interrupted again. "You hear, they let half the people down at the mill go yesterday? Paper's full of stories. Got an extra here somewhere." Ben twisted in his seat to find it, and turned back to the window. "Here we go, Mr. Coo—" He paused when he saw Cooper was gone, then shrugged and drove off along the road that wound through the valley. Its idyllic beauty belied the fact that, despite President Roosevelt's New Deal, much of rural America was still struggling to recover from the Depression.

Cooper set the package on the kitchen table, and snipped the twine, then began tearing at the wrapping like a starving man who'd just received a sack of groceries. The lettering on the shiny yellow box said: Eastman Kodak Company Orthochromatic Sheet Film. An anxious tingle rose in the pit of his stomach as he carried it into the crimson blackness of his darkroom where the stinging odor of chemicals reached full intensity. He ran a thumbnail along the edges to break the seal, then removed the black envelope, and opened the flap. His fingers found the edges of the celluloid sheets, and went about loading the double-sided film holders that he used with his view camera.

A short time later, he emerged from the cottage, looking somewhat like a door-to-door salesman burdened with his wares. A cracked leather bag stuffed with equipment hung from one shoulder, and his prized eight-by-ten Graflex affixed to a wooden tripod balanced on the other. Decades of service had given the finely crafted and elegantly simple instrument of metal, leather, glass, and wood the look of a burnished antique. Cooper pulled the door closed behind him, then paused and craned his neck skyward.

The sun burned softly behind clouds that the wind had sculpted into long lyrical wisps. Cooper studied them for a moment, then smiled approvingly and strode down the leaf-covered drive beneath bare, iron-gray trees that perfectly suited the hint of snow he sensed in the air.

Chapter Two

Newbury, the fishing village a few miles down the road from where Cooper lived, was on Ipswich Bay about forty miles north of Boston. Nestled amongst some of the most majestic coastal scenery in America, it had been built by people who were acutely sensitive to scale and proportion and paid careful attention to detail; but, of late, despite the warmth of crackling fires that sent graceful plumes curling from chimneys, and the snow flurries that made rooftops sparkle, its prim dwellings appeared tattered, and the people who lived in them seemed to have lost their sense of vitality and well-being.

Joe Clements drove down Main Street, as he did every morning, troubled by the Out Of Business signs that papered many of the storefronts. A lean man in his early thirties with chiseled features and neatly parted hair, Joe had lived in Newbury all his life and believed there was no better place to raise a family and run a business. He parked outside a shop where a sign proclaimed Clements & Son Printers, and smiled at the racket of the presses and linotypes that made the pavement vibrate beneath his feet—a racket he'd grown to love as a child. It served as a subtle reminder of how he had worked at his father's knee, sweeping floors, making deliveries, and learning the fine points of typography, the properties of papers and inks, and the need to treat employees and clients alike with fairness and respect.

Joe greeted his workers as he made his way between the clanking machines to his office, a small space separated from the work area by a mahogany and textured glass partition that muted the noise. Proofs of jobs that Clements & Son had run over the years—calendars, catalogues, business forms, posters, and everything in between—hung on the walls. In front of the window stood a stalwart oak desk piled with papers and a chair with tired leather cushions studded with brass tacks.

"Mornin', Mr. Clements," Lucas Bartlett said as Joe entered. An energetic fellow in his early twenties, he stood next to a pot-bellied stove warming his hands.

"Lucas," Joe said, hanging his mackinaw and scarf behind the door. "I hope this means you're finished."

Bartlett nodded and broke into a complacent grin, then handed him a thick manila envelope. It contained several dozen black-and-white photographs of hand tools and farming equipment.

Joe spread them out across the desk. "Good work, Lucas," he finally said. "Sharp, plenty of contrast. They'll make beautiful halftones."

"Yeah, I know. Mr. Mitchell was really tickled."

"Speaking of Ed," Joe said, surprised to see a balding paunchy fellow coming toward the office. "Ed, didn't expect you by today."

Mitchell brushed the snow from his coat as he entered, then pulled off a glove and shook Joe's hand. "Neither did I, I'm afraid."

"I was just telling Lucas, I think he did an excellent job on these."

Bartlett's chest filled with pride threatening to pop the buttons on his shirt. "They're the makings of the best Christmas catalogue Mitchell Hardware'll ever have, if I do say so myself."

Ed Mitchell nodded halfheartedly. "I thought so too. Unfortunately, the bank didn't agree."

The color began draining from Joe's face.

"They just turned down my loan," Mitchell went on. "I'm afraid I'm going to have to cancel the order."

"Cancel?" Joe gasped.

Mitchell's lips tightened into a thin line as he nodded. "I'm sorry. I've no choice, Joe. My business just went under."

"But we're running the job right now," Joe protested. "The halftones are all that's left."

Mitchell shrugged in frustration. "Care to tell me what I'm going to do with ten thousand mail order catalogues? I mean, you can print 'em if you want; but I'll never be able to pay you for 'em."

"What about the stock, inks, and plates? I mean, they're already bought and paid for, Ed. You're going to have to cover those expenses."

"I would if I could, Joe, but I'm bankrupt. Broke. There's nothing left."

Bartlett groaned and glanced to his photographs. "Nothing?"

"Nothing," Mitchell echoed. "I'm sorry. Believe me, I really am." He backed away a few steps, then turned, and hurried from the office.

Bartlett emitted a forlorn sigh. "Only work I had."

"You and me both," Joe said. He was staring at the photographs in disbelief when he sensed the silence and realized the racket in the shop had abated. He exchanged looks with Bartlett, then went to the doorway.

All the machinery was shut down.

His employees stood next to the suddenly stilled behemoths, staring at Joe with hopeless eyes. Foreman Gundersen; linotype operators Murphy and O'Hara; pressmen Benedetti, Lecont and Hendricks; and Porter, the kid who handled the paper cutter. They were all standing there, spirits broken, heads hanging, eyes taut with apprehension.

Joe swallowed hard, forced a smile, and went out onto the floor to reassure them.

Chapter Three

Cooper always thought the white clapboard bungalow that stood back from the beach beneath a stand of wind-shaped pines had a quiet dignity and seemed at peace with nature; and he'd always wanted to photograph it; but the angle of light, or patterns of shadow, or his mood, was never quite right. Not until this morning. Not until a brief flurry of powder-fine snow had given the scene a breathtaking crystalline sparkle.

The spiked legs of his tripod were set securely in the sand; and Cooper crouched behind the Graflex, the blackout cloth draped over his head, listening to the ebb and flow of the surf as he composed the picture. He extended the bellows, enhancing the trees with their swooping branches that embraced the bungalow as if protecting it, fine tuned the focus, then threw off the cloth, and inserted one of the film holders. He was about to fire the shutter when a young woman emerged from the bungalow, pulling on a coat. It struck him that something about her presence complemented the scene. So, he waited until she was just where he wanted her, then thumbed the cable release.

"Hello there," she called out as she approached. "I hope I didn't spoil your picture?"

"Nope," Cooper grunted. "I only fire that shutter when I want to."

"Well, good," she said brightly. "I've often seen you passing by and decided it was time to say hello. I'm Alicia. Alicia Clements."

"Cooper. Dylan Cooper. Dylan's more than enough."

Alicia smiled, then glanced curiously to the Graflex. "I've never seen a camera like that before. Not up close anyway." She squinted at it, and pointed to the lens. "What are the little numbers for?"

"They're called 'F' stops," he replied, grasping the serrated lens ring. The harsh daylight emphasized the coarseness of his hands and called attention to his fingernails which were cracked and totally blackened. "See that iris opening and closing in there?" he prompted as he clicked through the stops.

Alicia leaned closer to the lens and saw the overlapping steel blades stepping down in precise increments from a wide open position to a pinpoint.

"Just like the human eye," Cooper went on, clicking through them again. "It controls how much light gets to the film, among other things."

Alicia responded with a pensive nod, then crouched to the ground glass, and pulled the cloth over her head. "Hey?" she called out, her voice ringing with surprise. "Everything's upside down in here?"

"It'll take me till tomorrow to explain that to you," Cooper replied with an amused grin.

Alicia reappeared from beneath the cloth. "That's okay. I've got plenty of time."

Cooper glanced to the sky. "Well, I'm afraid I don't. Take my word for it. It all comes out right side up when it's done." Another anxious glance to the sky heightened his sense of urgency. "Just about where I want it. But not for long."

"What do you mean?"

"The light. I'm either sitting around waitin' for it, or I'm chasin' after it." He gestured to her bulging tummy and, letting his burr thicken with charm, added, "Rather like having a baby, I imagine."

Alicia chuckled, clearly taken by him. A wholesome woman of simple beauty, she was in her seventh month and her skin had taken on a lush radiance.

"Sorry to be hurrying off like this." Cooper bent to the camera, gathered the legs of the tripod and tilted it onto his shoulder. "This time of year, I'm always on the lookout for a special Christmas picture."

"Oh, I hope you find it," Alicia said, pulling her coat around her against the cold.

"I always do," Cooper said with a mysterious twinkle. "And I've been doing it every year for as long as I can remember." He smiled and started off down the beach, bent beneath the weight of the equipment that sent each step deep into the sand.

Chapter Four

The Clements's bungalow was heated by a cast-iron furnace in the basement along with a stone fireplace in the parlor. The latter was tastefully furnished with a floral patterned sofa, several wicker easy chairs on opposite sides of a coffee table, a wall of bookcases, and a rolltop desk where Joe sat poring over bills and invoices that were getting the best of him.

"Time for a break," Alicia announced, bringing him a cup of coffee. "I just made it."

"Thanks," Joe said glumly, reviewing the bills. "We had a coal delivery this week?"

Alicia nodded. "Everyone's saying it's going to be a long winter. Best to make sure the bin is full."

"We still have to pay for it." He sipped his coffee, then went to a window. A crescent moon hung in the darkness, dappling the sea with silver-blue light.

Alicia drifted after him and ran her palm across his back. "It'll be okay, darling. It will."

"It's hard to believe, after what happened today."

"You're not being fair to yourself, Joe. This isn't the first order you've had cancelled."

"True, but what's going on in the rest of the country is going on in Newbury too. These are bad times. No time to be starting a family."

Alicia forced a comical frown; then cradled her tummy. "I

hope he didn't hear you. He'll come into this world thinking he isn't wanted."

"Hey, no jokes, okay?" Joe fetched a sheet of paper from the desk and held it up to her. "One new order—one—unconfirmed. If I lose it, I'm out of business."

Alicia's jaw slackened. "I didn't realize it was that bad. I mean, it's the—"

"Well, it is!" Joe snapped, wishing he could take it back the instant he'd said it. "I'm sorry. I don't mean to take it out on you; but I'll have to close up at the end of the month and . . . and let everyone go."

"Oh, Joseph, no," Alicia groaned. "I'd no idea. I mean, it's the first time you mentioned it."

"Wasn't any sense worrying you." He dropped into the desk chair and took a long swallow of coffee.

"When will you hear about that order?"

"Tomorrow. I'm taking the train down to Boston."

Alicia wrapped her arms around him. "You'll get it, Joe. I know you will."

Joe stared at his coffee for a moment; then, still far from convinced that she was right, he leaned against the gentle swell of her stomach and looked up at her. "I love you," he whispered.

"I love you too," she said, kissing his forehead. "Don't worry, it'll all work out."

Joe nodded morosely.

"It will," Alicia said. "Did you notice the poinsettias in the yard have already started to bud?"

"No, what's that have to do with this?"

"The holidays, Joe. Things seem to have a way of working out at this time of year." Alicia said it with as much conviction as she could muster; but it was clear the business was in serious difficulty and she was deeply concerned.

Chapter Five

The next morning, after dropping Joe at the train station, Alicia drove to the Town Square and parked their roadster in front of a house where a neatly lettered shingle proclaimed: Edward F. Cheever, M.D.

Doctor Cheever had been caring for the people of Newbury for more than thirty years, and had brought many of them into the world, Alicia among them. After a routine examination, he peered over his rimless spectacles, declared that mommy and baby were doing fine, and sent Alicia on her way.

The doctor's stately fieldstone house was just across the square from the Newbury Community Church. It was sheathed in white-painted clapboard and topped by a steeple that soared into the autumn foliage above; and as Alicia went to her car, her attention was drawn to the spirited singing that was coming from within.

"God rest ye merry gentlemen,
Let nothing you dismay . . .
Remember Christ our Savior,
Was born on Christmas day . . ."

Alicia paused in reflection. She had been a member of the choir as a teenager and a regular at weekly services with her parents who gave generously of their time and what little money they could spare; but after their passing Alicia's commitment to her church waned.

Now, humming the carol to herself, she hurried past the roadster and across the square to the church.

The pastor was clapping his hands to silence the choir as Alicia entered. "You're rushing the tempo. Slow down, savor the words, extend the phrases fully," he instructed before sweeping his hands in a graceful arc and the church filled with soaring voices.

Alicia slipped into one of the pews near the back and knelt in prayer. She prayed that her baby would be born healthy as Dr. Cheever said, then said a special prayer that Joe's business meeting would go well. She became so caught up in her hopes, fears and thoughts that she didn't realize choir practice had ended until she felt a hand on her shoulder.

"Alicia?" the pastor said, pleased to see her.

"Oh, Pastor Martin," Alicia exclaimed in surprise. "The choir . . . it sounds just . . . just wonderful."

"Well, we still miss your cheerful soprano," he said, sounding as if he meant it. A slight fellow with sparkling eyes and gray-flecked hair, he had been the pastor here for more than three decades. "We miss you at Sunday services too."

Alicia nodded in contrition. "Well, between keeping house and helping out with the business and now the baby coming, the days just seem to get filled."

Pastor Martin absolved her with a smile. "Speaking of the business, how's Joe doing these days?"

"Working harder than ever. He'll soon have another mouth to feed," Alicia replied, forcing a laugh; then her eyes clouded and she added, "Business has been terrible, Pastor Martin. He's . . . he's been talking about closing the shop."

"Oh, I'm sorry to hear that," Pastor Martin said. "But I can't say I'm surprised. So many of our parishioners are struggling to get by. I remind them that God has a plan for each of us; and these tough times are undoubtedly part of it. A test perhaps."

Alicia nodded, then her eyes filled. "Will you say a prayer that Joe gets this order he's after?"

"Of course, I will. Why don't you both come by one day. I can't save Joe's business, but I might be able to raise his spirits."

"I'm sure you could, but you know Joe . . . he isn't much of a churchgoer."

The Pastor's eyes narrowed. "The last time was the day I married you, if I'm not mistaken."

Alicia nodded and glanced to her tummy. "And the next will be for the christening, I imagine."

"Well, don't you be a stranger," Pastor Martin said. "And don't give up on Joe. We'll soon be celebrating the birth of Jesus. God sent Him to redeem us all, Alicia. I don't recall anything in the Bible excluding men from Newbury who aren't churchgoers."

Chapter Six

Just down the beach from the Clements's bungalow, a massive rock formation cut through the tidal pools in a sweeping arc that extended into the sea. For millennia, the windward face had been pounded smooth by angry surf, while the leeward, gently lapped by harbor waters, had remained craggy and untouched. Cooper was drawn to the contrast and photographed it often: at dawn, at dusk, at the height of thunderstorms, and raging blizzards; and, today, in wintry fog, his Graflex aimed at a dock where a weathered rowboat which had been pulled out for the winter, lay upside down on the salt-stained decking. He racked the bellows back and forth, bringing the vessel's craggy hull into sharp focus, then made his exposure. The snap of the shutter segued to a voice.

"Hello up there?"

Cooper turned and looked down to see Alicia bundled against the cold, waving a mittened hand. She had just returned home from the doctor's and her impromptu church visit and spotted the old fellow as she got out of her car.

"Well, hello," Cooper said, pleasantly surprised, as he clambered off the rocks and joined her. "Sorry, I couldn't chat longer yesterday. You sure seemed to be full of questions."

Alicia nodded emphatically. "I still am."

Cooper had sensed this inevitability and broke into a knowing smile. "Answer 'em as best I can."

"Okay. Will you tell me what makes you haul that heavy camera around day after day?"

"Well," Cooper mused, "I could say since the Depression there isn't much else to do anyway. But it's simpler than that. It's what I do. Dylan Cooper was put on this earth to take pictures."

"You certainly sound sure of that."

"Aye. I'm positive."

"Since when? I mean, when did you know?"

Cooper's eyes took on a mischievous glint. "I guess when I sold my sister's bicycle to buy my first camera. Caught a nasty caning for that one, I did. My bottom stung for a week."

Alicia chuckled heartily.

Cooper laughed along with her, then glanced to his equipment. "Time for me to be going, if I'm ever going to get to work on these negatives."

Alicia's eyes widened with curiosity.

"I'm afraid, there's no time for questions about that, now," Cooper added before she could ask.

"Okay. No questions," Alicia said, undaunted. "Suppose I just tag along and watch?"

"Nothing to see. It's all done in darkness."

"Really? That sounds fascinating."

"It's a small space. There's only room for one."

"But you've taken pictures of my bungalow and my boat," Alicia pleaded. "I just want to see what happens next. I think it's only fair, don't you?"

"*Your* boat?" Cooper asked, changing the subject.

Alicia nodded proudly. The dinghy had been built in the classic New England style with brass oarlocks and a hull of lapstrake planking that formed a graceful curve at the prow. "It was my father's," she replied. "He was a lobsterman. Worked these waters for nearly fifty years. He taught me to row when I was nine. Same boat as a matter of fact. We're old friends."

"Ah, they're the best kind, aren't they?"

"And what does that mean?" she asked, a hint of indignation creeping into her voice.

"It means they're dependable, loyal. You can count on them, and they can count on you." Cooper's burr thickened with charm. "Of course, they all start out as new ones, don't they?"

"They certainly do," Alicia replied, pleased by the gesture. "You live nearby?"

"Up the hill a ways," he replied.

"We can take my car if you like, it'll be faster."

Cooper thought it over for a moment, then nodded. He gathered his equipment, and a short time later they were settled in the roadster, winding up the road that led from the coast to Cooper's place.

He headed straight for the darkroom upon arrival. It had once been the garage, but the mild odor of gas and oil had long been replaced by the heady blend of bromides, sulfites, and hydroquinone. "Sit over there, and don't be underfoot," Cooper growled as if to a child. He wasted no time developing his negatives; and now, while they were drying, he fetched the one he'd taken of the bungalow yesterday and stepped to a small table where he made his prints.

Alicia perched on the stool to which she'd been assigned, watching as he cleaned the negative with a soft brush. When satisfied it was free of dust, he placed it atop an eight-by-ten sheet of Royal Velox—the photographic paper he favored because of its rich luster and fine gradation quality—and covered it with a piece of glass which kept the surfaces in contact; then he grasped a length of beaded chain hanging from a light fixture directly above the table. "Ready?"

Alicia nodded.

Cooper pulled on the chain.

The switch emitted a loud click, the bare bulb came to life, and Cooper began counting.

Alicia squinted at the blinding glare and looked about curiously. They'd been working in red-tinged blackness from the start, and this was her first look at the darkroom. The walls, ceiling and floor were painted black. A long table along one wall held three enameled trays filled with chemicals that had the clarity of water. Above the table, yellow boxes of printing papers were stacked neatly on shelves. Below, brown bottles of chemicals with matching yellow labels and graduated measuring beakers stood in wooden racks. The sound of trickling water came from a sink at the far end where a number of negatives were still washing. Alicia was thinking: stark, efficient, organized, not a speck of dust anywhere when the light switch clicked and the room was suddenly plunged back into darkness.

Cooper removed the sheet of glass, separated the negative and print, and slipped the latter into the tray of developer.

Alicia's curiosity got the best of her. She left the stool and crept up next to him, watching as the chemical did its work. The wind-shaped trees that framed the bungalow were the first images to emerge. "You sure I didn't spoil it?"

"No, of course not," Cooper replied as her figure appeared in the foreground of the photograph. "There you are. Aye, it's a fine picture." He was gently rocking the tray, coaxing every nuance of tone and texture from the print when the muffled ring of a telephone came from somewhere in the cottage. Cooper ignored it, letting it ring and ring. "They'll call back if it's important," he said, continuing to rock the tray until the blacks had attained the richness of velvet, and the whites the crystalline sparkle of the snow that dusted the trees. Then he offered a pair of wooden tongs to Alicia. "Now, by the corner; and careful, that stuff blackens everything it touches, especially fingernails."

Alicia glanced with apprehension from his hands to hers, then gingerly transferred the print to the stop bath, an acid which neutralized the developer on contact and arrested the process.

"That's it," Cooper said, encouraging her. He rocked the tray to ensure the print was submerged, and left it there for a few moments. "Okay, now into the last one. It has to stay in there for a while."

"Why?"

"It's a special chemical that fixes the image in the paper. Makes it permanent."

"Photographers have to know a lot about chemistry, don't they?"

Cooper shook his head no. "Not really. I don't have half the knowledge my father did."

"Oh, then I imagine he was either a pharmacist or chemistry professor, wasn't he?"

"Neither, I'm afraid. Not that he wasn't keen enough, mind you; but no, he was apprenticed to the mills as a boy. Learned his craft and worked his way up. A dyemaster, he was. All the wools had to pass his inspection. He could pick out the slightest imperfection in color or tone; had the most incredible eye." Cooper paused in reflection, then covered the tray that held the finished print and opened the door. "Now, what do you say to some tea and biscuits?"

"They have to smell better than these chemicals."

"I've never been able to make up my mind about that," Cooper said without a hint of levity as he showed Alicia into the parlor. "Make yourself comfortable. I'll just be a few minutes."

In marked contrast to the darkroom, it was dusty and cluttered and lacked a woman's touch. The windows were without curtains, the upholstery threadbare, and the floors unwaxed. Books were stuffed into rickety cases and piled on every surface; various photogenic objects—rusted machinery, twisted pieces of driftwood, sun-bleached bones, dried flowers—were scattered about, along with unopened mail, newspapers, copies of the *National Geographic* magazine, and potted plants that begged to be watered.

Alicia frowned at their droopy leaves and rock-hard soil. She was about to follow Cooper into the kitchen to fetch some water and give them a lifesaving drink when the photographs that literally papered the walls caught her eye: pictures of Newbury with its snug harbor and fishing boats. Of its houses, farms and shops. Its sawmills and canneries. Its snowcapped mountains and lush forests. Its pastoral landscapes and raging sea. And its townsfolk. Pictures of tradesmen, field hands, fishermen, blacksmiths, and bankers; of schoolteachers and loggers; of rugged faces, weathered hands, and weary eyes. Each black-and-white print had a powerful vision and sparkling luminosity that made it all the more moving, all the more breathtaking; and it dawned on Alicia that though the people and places had been part of her life for more than twenty-five years, she'd never really seen them before; never been aware of their inherent beauty and poetic themes.

She was lost in her thoughts when she came upon several whose subject matter wasn't at all familiar. Taken from the air, they were displayed above the fireplace where an aviator's scuffed helmet and pitted goggles hung from a nail. A snapshot of uniformed flyers, posing in front of an open cockpit biplane, hung next to them. Alicia was studying it when Cooper returned with a tray that, along with biscuits, teapot, and china, held a bottle of whiskey.

"This is you, isn't it?" Alicia prompted, pointing to one of the men in the snapshot.

"Aye," Cooper grunted. He placed the tray on an upside down packing crate that served as a table. "The funny looking frightened one in the middle."

Alicia emitted a fetching chuckle. "Frightened? I've always thought of flyers as fearless and handsome."

"Oh, that they were," Cooper replied, basking in the compliment. "But I wasn't a flyer, you see. I was assigned to an aerial reconnaissance unit. We'd go up, over enemy territory, and I'd hang over the side with my camera and take pictures of the ground."

Alicia hugged herself and shivered at the thought. "Oh, I'd be frightened too."

"Aye, I was glad when the war was over and I could get back home; back to . . . to—" Cooper almost said, to my wife, but paused, deciding whether or not he'd share it with her. "—back to taking pictures of whatever happens to catch my eye." He sipped his tea in reflection, then seemed to stiffen with anger. "Something about being told what to photograph has never sat right with me. Cost me a job once."

"You mean you were fired?" Alicia prompted.

Cooper's eyes flared as if he'd been insulted. "I quit," he snapped. Then sensing he'd startled her, he gently explained, "It was years ago. I was exhibiting at one of those fancy Beacon Hill galleries at the time. The reviews were . . ."

"In Boston?" Alicia asked, sounding impressed.

Cooper nodded. "The Van Dusen. One of the best. The reviews were quite favorable, as I recall. I had visions of fame and fortune, of my work being acquired by museums and private collectors . . ."

"So what happened?" Alicia asked, hearing the disappointment in his voice.

"Nothing. Didn't sell a picture. Not even one. It seems the carriage trade didn't think photographs were investment grade art." Cooper chortled at what he was about to say, then added, "I was broke, in debt, and being evicted from my rooming house."

"That's where the job comes in, doesn't it?" Alicia prompted.

Cooper nodded smartly. "Aye. I took on an assignment—a commercial assignment—fashion photography. I even convinced a young lady I was sweet on to model for me."

Alicia's brows arched with intrigue. "I see."

"Aye, and commercial work or no, the pictures were magnificent," Cooper went on, caught up in the memory. "I was bursting with pride when I delivered them to the client. You know what he did?"

"I can't imagine," Alicia replied, apprehensively.

"He rejected them. That's what! The fool claimed that they were too artistic; that—that the model was too exotic. He actually had the gall to show me someone else's pictures—uninspired, pedestrian trash—as an example of what he wanted." Then in a burr thicker than the molasses he sometimes spooned into his tea, Cooper boomed, "And you know why?! Because he thought they'd sell more bonnets! Well, that's when I headed for the door. All he was interested in was making money! Unprincipled son of a—agghhh!" Cooper groaned with disgust. "Enough of that nonsense."

Alicia was taken by his intensity, and could only nod in response. They settled into overstuffed chairs that faced each other across the packing crate. Cooper poured two cups of tea. "Lemon?"

"Please," Alicia replied, smiling at what she was about to say. "But not too bitter."

"Oh, clever aren't you?" Cooper bristled, stung by her insight. "But oh, no. No, that I'm not. Not bitter a'tall." He squeezed some lemon into Alicia's tea, then poured some whiskey into his own. "As it turns out, Mr. Van Dusen was a very supportive fellow. Suggested I send my pictures to the National Geographic Society. They ended up buying every one of 'em; and I ended up buying this cottage. Best part is, they've been buying 'em on and off, ever since."

"Well," Alicia said with a sip of her tea, "things have a way of working out, don't they?" She set the cup down, and went about spreading marmalade on a biscuit.

Cooper's face brightened as he watched her. "You know, I'm

really enjoying this. I mean, it isn't often I have a young visitor to spar with."

"I'm rather enjoying it too. It's the first time I've ever made friends with—" She paused, realizing she was about to say something she shouldn't. "Well, I mean, I've never known—"

Cooper laughed and interrupted. "An old man?"

Alicia reddened with embarrassment. "I'm sorry. I didn't mean to—Well, I guess that is what I was going to say."

"Well, I guess I am old to someone of your tender years. But maybe we can be a little more charitable than that. How about . . ." Cooper paused and searched for an appropriate description. "Someone who's managed a fair amount of livin', and is showin' a bit of wear?"

Alicia considered it and smiled. "I think I could accept that." She took a sip of tea, then glanced at her watch. "Oh my," she exclaimed. "I seem to have lost track of time." She jumped to her feet, made her apologies, and headed for the door, pulling on her coat.

"I'll bring the picture by tomorrow," Cooper called out as she got into the roadster.

"Why don't you come for dinner?"

Cooper wrestled with it briefly. "Why not?"

"Good," Alicia exclaimed. "Six-thirty." She drove off with a wave, then glanced back over her shoulder and shouted, "Your plants need watering!"

Cooper stood at the gate and waved back. Alicia's sudden departure had left him with misty eyes and a vast emptiness that brought on an alarming surge of emotion. It wasn't that he was smitten, which of course he was, but that the feelings she stirred had been dormant for so long; feelings that, though crushed by life's vicissitudes, had steadfastly refused to die; and, now, as the bittersweet memories surfaced, Grace's lithe figure pirouetted in the bubbling surf; and her contagious laugh echoed off the hills;

and then, for the briefest of moments, her fragrance filled his head, replacing the stinging scent of chemicals.

It had been twenty years since Cooper had left his bride to go off to war; but, it wasn't the memory of their poignant farewell at a Boston trolley stop that had so powerfully touched him, but of his painful homecoming almost a year later; and, now, as if it were yesterday, he recalled how he had returned to their cottage in Newbury, expecting to find his beloved Grace and their newly born child waiting for him, only to learn from her brother, Colin, of the tragic events that had caused Grace to return to Scotland.

Cooper's anguish at the heartbreaking news—that she had lost the baby and that a telegram stating he'd been killed in action had emotionally devastated her—had been tempered by time, but never forgotten; nor, despite his immediate return to Scotland and the months he'd spent in a frustrating and finally futile search for Grace, had he ever forsaken his vow to find her. Indeed, for two decades now, his heart had kept the hope alive; but she had long ago slipped away, and he'd since lived alone with the emptiness.

Chapter Seven

The sun always set directly behind Newbury's train station at this time of year. It framed the steep roof against a pewter sky, and made the tracks shimmer like polished silver. The afternoon local from Boston had already come and gone; and the few passengers who'd gotten off had long ago headed home. All except one.

In fedora and woollen overcoat, Joe Clements stood inside the unheated station, keeping one eye on the parking area, the other on a newspaper. The headline read: Economic Recovery Expected To Be Slow. The story stated that despite the Public Works Programs funded by Congress, it would be years before small businesses and rural communities were expected to benefit. Joe sighed and glanced at his watch with impatience. His eyes were drifting to another story about the massing of German troops along the western border of Poland when he heard a vehicle approaching. The station's old window panes distorted the scene beyond, but it was undoubtedly their roadster.

"Sorry I'm late, darling," Alicia said as Joe got in next to her.

"I've only been waiting a few minutes," he said coolly, kissing her cheek.

"Good," Alicia chirped, oblivious to his mood. "It's a long story. I'll tell you on the way."

Minutes later, they were racing along the beach road toward the bungalow. Alicia talked above the roar of the motor, punctuating her bubbly chatter with shift changes and bursts of acceleration: "Of course, he wasn't very keen on the idea—and it took a little coaxing—but I finally talked him into letting me come along."

"Uh-huh," Joe muttered distantly.

"He's really an amazing old fellow."

"I'll bet."

"His name's Cooper. Dylan Cooper. We printed a photograph of the bungalow. I just lost track of time."

"I said I only waited a few minutes, Alicia," Joe said indulgently. "It's okay."

"Then we had biscuits and tea and just talked and talked . . . and . . ."

"Better turn on your lights."

"What?"

"Your lights."

"Lights? Oh, lights." Alicia flipped the switch, then shifted down a gear, and guided the car into a sharp turn. The headlights swept across the road and flickered between the bare trees, painting the darkness a soft yellow. "Wait till you see it," she resumed without missing a beat. "The picture, I mean. It's really beautiful. He said he would—"

"I'm sure it's very nice."

"Oh, it is. He said he'd bring it by tomorrow. So I asked him to dinner. I hope that's okay?"

"Well, I suppose. I mean—"

"Good. I know you're going to—"

"Alicia?" Joe interrupted gently.

"I know, you're going to like him," she charged on undaunted. "He's—"

"Alicia?!" Joe said, his tone sharpening. "Alicia, I wish you'd listen."

"Oh, sure. What is it?"

"You just drove past the house."

"Oh my goodness!" She hit the brakes, made a U-turn, and headed back toward the bungalow. "I just got so wrapped up in my story that I—"

"Really?" Joe snapped. "I hadn't noticed."

"Pardon me?!" Alicia exclaimed, stung by his tone. She pulled the car into the drive behind the bungalow. It had barely come to a stop when Joe opened the door to get out. "Not so fast, Clements," she said, stopping him. "Now, what was that all about?"

"Well, to be brutally frank, Alicia, you haven't stopped talking since I got in the car; and right now, I need a listener."

Alicia nodded in apology. "Your meeting . . . you want to tell me about your meeting, don't you? You know," she raced on before Joe could utter a word, "I stopped in at church after Dr. Cheever's this morning and I—"

"Church?" Joe's tone had a disapproving timbre. "What's church got to do with this?"

"Well, I said a prayer that your meeting would go well and you'd get that order."

"So much for the power of prayer," Joe snapped.

"I guess that means you . . . you . . ." The words caught in her throat and she took a deep breath before continuing. ". . . You didn't get it?"

"No, Alicia, I didn't."

"I'm sorry. I guess I just didn't want to hear it."

"Neither did I, believe me," Joe retorted.

Alicia's shoulders sagged. She'd been hoping beyond hope that he would reply to the contrary; and the disappointment and sense of failure in his eyes nearly moved her to tears. She reached out and touched his face. They sat there in silence, hugging each other, then went inside.

Alicia took a few moments to pull herself together, then washed her face with cold water and went about preparing dinner. She was setting the table when she noticed Joe at the desk, staring at the pile of bills. "How about taking in a movie, to-night?" she suggested, trying to cheer him.

Joe lit a cigarette in silence.

"Joe?"

"We can't afford it."

"I know, but *Animal Crackers* is playing, and—"

"The Marx Brothers?" Joe interrupted, his mood brighten-ing somewhat.

"Uh-huh. I think we should go."

"We'll see," he mumbled as he exhaled, filling the space be-tween them with smoke.

Like its church and train station, Newbury's movie theater had an inviting charm; and for ninety minutes, Joe, Alicia, and a capacity crowd of townsfolk sat in red velvet seats and doubled over with laughter at the madcap antics; at Groucho's African lecture—"One morning I shot an elephant in my pajamas. How he got into my pajamas I'll never know!" And at the side-splitting humor of Harpo's bridge game; and when the image faded, and the house lights came up, the audience headed for the exits, buzzing with renewed vitality.

"Well," Alicia said brightly as they huddled against the cold and crossed the street to the roadster. "You seem to be feeling a little better."

"I am. It was a good idea. Thanks."

Joe had just gotten her settled in the car when the newsstand on the corner caught his eye. "Be right back." He closed the door and hurried off, joining the crowd that surged around the kiosk.

The dealer was doing a brisk business in newspapers and magazines: *Liberty, Colliers, Life, The Saturday Evening Post* were the bestsellers among the latter. The front page stories ranged from the World's Fair in New York to the advent of war in Europe. The slight fellow chatted amiably with customers, most of whom he greeted by name, while his ink-smudged fingers made change with amazing speed and dexterity, darting in and out of the pockets of his apron that bulged with pennies, nickles, dimes, and quarters respectively.

Joe spotted a copy of *Life* and quickly plucked it from the rack, then paid for it and sauntered back toward the car where Alicia sat watching the action, quietly entertaining an idea that had occurred to her.

Chapter Eight

He'd already showered, shaved, and dressed for work, but Joe Clements was anything but ready to face this day. He sat in the breakfast nook that overlooked the beach, stirring his coffee, and thumbing through the magazine he'd purchased the night before; though, at the moment, he had little interest in it.

Alicia was the one who found it intriguing. Hands wrapped around her cup to warm them, she watched as page after page of pictures went by; then glanced out the frosty window, reflecting on the idea she'd had last night. A wind had come up, rattling the shutters, and whipping the sea into a frenzy that sent waves crashing over the tiny dock.

"Well," Joe said in a morose tone, "I guess, I can't put it off any longer, can I?"

"Put off what?" Alicia wondered, still lost in her thoughts.

"The people in the shop. Today's the day."

"Today? So soon?"

"Good as any other day. It's only right to give them fair warning."

"Oh no," Alicia sighed, turning up the collar of her robe against the chill. "I'm sorry."

"I mean, some of them have been there since before I was born. A few actually began with Dad. He gave them Christmas bonuses this time of year. I'll be giving them pink slips. I was up half the night worrying about it."

"I know," she said softly, taking his hand in hers.

"And I still haven't figured out how to break it to them." He leaned back, staring at the ceiling in search of the answer.

"Well . . ." Alicia mused, her eyes drifting back to the window while she decided if she'd continue. "Maybe . . . Maybe you won't have to, Joe."

"I won't?" he wondered, mystified. "What do you mean? You going to do it for me?"

"No. I have an idea. I'm not sure about it, but with God's help, it might work."

"God?" Joe echoed with a sarcastic snicker. "Since when did you two become such pals?"

"Since you and I used to steal glances at each other at Sunday school," Alicia replied with a smile. "Under the circumstances, it seemed like a good time to get back in touch with Him."

"So what did He have to say?"

"Well, according to Pastor Martin, we should accept these difficult times as part of His plan. You remember the lesson about God having a plan for everyone? That it's up to each of us to trust in Him to reveal it to us?"

"Yeah, well, when it comes to Clements & Son Printers, it seems God's plan is to put a lot of decent people out of work."

"Joe, I know you're upset that you didn't get that order," Alicia resumed, undaunted, "but maybe it isn't part of the Plan. I can't be sure, but maybe, just maybe, this idea I have is. It wouldn't cost anything to hear me out."

"I'm sorry. Go ahead."

Alicia reached across the table and picked up the copy of *Life* magazine. "How many of these do you think that newsdealer sold last night?"

"Dozens. He couldn't make change fast enough."

Alicia nodded emphatically. "Right. And neither could the ticket seller at the movies. I'll bet half the people in that theater were out of work. And the other half facing financial difficulty of some kind."

"No question about it."

"But they were still there, weren't they?"

"Sure were," Joe conceded, curiously. He pulled a cigarette from the pack with his lips and lit it. "What does that have to do with the business?"

"My point is that people are spending the little money they have on things that will help them forget the misery in their lives; things that will take them to another place, a better time. Think about it." She put the copy of *Life* back in front of him. "This magazine didn't exist a few years ago. It was born in bad times, Joe, but it survived; it's doing well. And from the look of things, it's not the only one. I guess what I'm saying is, the printing business isn't dead. What's dead is business printing."

Joe nodded thoughtfully, struck by her incisive observation. "I can't argue with that; but we're a small shop with limited capacity, miles from where that kind of material is published. No one's going to give us an order to print a national magazine. Our work has always come from local sources."

"Exactly," Alicia exclaimed with a broad grin. "And I've got one for you."

"You do?"

"Dylan Cooper, my photographer friend. I did tell you he's coming to dinner, didn't I?"

Joe nodded, then his brow furrowed with confusion. "But how does he fit into this?"

"Well, while he's here, I think you should talk to him about publishing a book; a book of—"

Joe looked incredulous. "A book?"

"Uh-huh. A book of his pictures. His Christmas pictures. He said he takes a special one every year."

Joe stared at her dumbfounded. "Alicia, I'm not a publisher. I don't know the first thing about it. Not to mention that—"

"That's okay," she interrupted, gesturing to her bulging tummy. "I've never been a mother before either. What makes you think you can't learn?"

"That's different. Something like this could take the last of our savings."

"Well, as I recall, you do have the paper and inks left over from Ed Mitchell's job, don't you?"

"True. Still, we could end up with thousands of copies of that book in the shop and nothing in the bank. Besides, why do you think anyone would buy it?"

"Because I've seen Dylan's pictures, Joe. They're good, really good. He's been photographing this area for thirty years." She got to her feet, her voice rising with enthusiasm and a sense of awe, and resumed: "The mountains cloaked in mist; fishing boats at sunrise; winding lanes carpeted with leaves; Main Street with horses and buggies; the harbor blanketed in snow. Other places, better times, Joe. I'm convinced people around here would buy a book like that. And there are thousands of them . . ." She let it trail off, then found Joe's eyes with hers, and added, "And Christmas is just a few months away."

Joe leaned back in the chair, sorting it out. He'd always been taken by her resourcefulness and spunk. They were teenagers when he first experienced it. She was working after school in the local bakery at the time. The stern Dutch proprietor had a rule that only broken cookies be given to customers as samples; and one day, when Joe stopped by to flirt with Alicia and help himself to some free samples, the jar was empty. She discreetly smashed several of his favorites with her fist and slipped them beneath the lid. "It's not empty now," she said with a mischievous giggle. That was the moment he fell in love with her; and ever since, when he was beaten, she was undaunted; when he lost his way, she somehow found it; and when he ran out of ideas, she always managed to come up with one.

Now, Joe looked at her with a mixture of wary interest, and renewed hope. "You're really serious, aren't you?"

"Yes, I am," Alicia replied in her spirited way. "I have a good feeling about Dylan—about this idea. I think he'd be very receptive to it."

Chapter Nine

"Nope. Not interested," Cooper said with finality.

Joe forced a smile. "Well, I guess I got my answer, didn't I?"

"Aye. That you did."

"Well, it's not the one I was hoping for, I'm afraid. Perhaps, if I explained it more clearly . . ."

"Nope," Cooper grunted, unmoved. He drew on his pipe, emitting a stream of smoke that rose in graceful twists to the bungalow's peaked ceiling. "Christmas pictures or no, a book's just not in the cards for me."

"I don't see why not," Joe said, glancing to Alicia in search of support.

She was standing to one side of the crackling fire hanging Cooper's poetic photograph of the bungalow. He had set the print in a simple black frame that didn't compete with it for attention; and Alicia wasted no time fetching a hammer and nail from a drawer in the kitchen and finding just the right spot for it.

She was so intent on what she was doing that she seemed not to have noticed Joe's plaintive glance, though she had. Indeed, instead of acknowledging him, she was tilting the picture frame this way and that, making certain it was straight, and using the time to work out her strategy. "Well?" she finally prompted, stepping aside so they could see it.

"Perfect," Joe said.

Cooper's eyes narrowed. "A little lower on the left, Alicia."

Alicia smiled and made the adjustment. "You were right, Dylan. It's a *fine* picture," she said in her brightest voice. "Isn't it, Joe?"

"Oh, yes," Joe replied preoccupied. "Certainly is."

Alicia crossed the room and settled on the sofa opposite Cooper. "I guess I owe you an apology," she said in a matter-of-fact tone.

Cooper's brows went up as she anticipated. "Do you, now?"

"Uh-huh. You see, this was all my doing," she replied, further embellishing the mystery.

"And what might it be that was your doing?"

"The book. I mean, I'm the one who suggested to Joe that he talk to you about it."

Cooper toyed with his pipe stem. "Really, I'd no idea," he said with a wily smile. "Now, why would you do such a thing?"

"Because I thought you'd be interested in having a book of your Christmas pictures published; and if we did it in time for the holidays, I have a feeling it would be very—"

"Well, I'm not," Cooper interrupted, his burr taking on an abrasive edge. "And if *that's* the reason you invited me to dinner, then we'd best forget that, too." He jammed his pipe hard into the corner of his mouth, pulled himself from the chair, and lumbered across the room, scooping his well-worn mackinaw from the coat rack that stood near the door.

"Dylan?" Alicia called out. "Dylan, wait!"

Cooper paused and looked back at her, then tugged the pipe from between his teeth and fired his parting shot. "Like I said, old friends are the best kind."

Alicia flinched, stung by his words and the cocky thrust of his jaw which he used to remind her that she knew all too well what he meant; but instead of taking offense, Alicia saw beyond the insult and the anger, and there was compassion not retaliation, in her eyes.

Cooper saw the emotion in them and, flushed with remorse, was not at all pleased with what he'd just done. "I suppose if I was really honest with myself, I'd have to admit it is something I've thought about on occasion."

Alicia broke into a knowing smile.

Cooper took a moment to regain his composure. "I guess, if I'm going to do something about it, I shouldn't wait too long, should I?"

"Oh, Dylan, don't say that," Alicia replied, guiding him to his chair. "You're—"

"I'm sixty-two, that's what I am," Cooper bellowed, unwilling to take his seat. "And when you get that far into the tunnel, you start seeing the other end pretty clear." He fidgeted self-consciously, then as if confiding in them, said, "You know, I take most of my pictures in my mind first, or at least I think I do, and lately I—" His voice broke and he faltered briefly. "Lately, I keep seeing this one picture, and I'm in it—me, and . . . and—" He paused, then dismissed it with a wave of his hand. "Well, that one won't be in the book, will it?"

The question hung there unanswered, the silence filled by the crackling that came from the fireplace.

Alicia caught Joe's eye and prompted him with a nod.

"So, Mr. Cooper," he began.

"Dylan."

"Dylan," Joe repeated. "Am I to take that to mean you've changed your mind?"

"No," Cooper replied, his tone sharpening. "It means I've decided to speak it." He looked Joe square in the eye, taking his measure of him. "If we're going to do this, Joe, I want to do it right. What do you know about publishing books?"

Joe held the old fellow's gaze for a moment. There was only

one answer. "Not a thing." He glanced to Alicia, then added, "But I'm willing to work day and night to learn."

Cooper tamped his pipe. "Well, you won't be the first fellow to do something who didn't know a thing about it when he started. I like people who are forthright, Joe. I think you and I are going to get along."

"So do I."

"Good. Now, would you mind telling me why you want to do this book?"

"Of course not. To make money. Right now, nothing's more important to me than keeping my business from going under."

Cooper's eyes hardened momentarily, then they took on a mischievous gleam and shifted to Alicia. "He sounds like a publisher already, if you ask me."

Alicia erupted with laughter.

Joe smiled good-naturedly and waited as Cooper took his seat. "All kidding aside, Dylan," he said as the painted wicker shifted and creaked. "I think we should get this issue settled right now."

"So do I. Besides, I've a feeling dinner'll be far more enjoyable if we do. Proceed."

"You want something and I want something, right?"

"Good a way as any of putting it."

"The way I see it, there's nothing wrong with making money from your book as long as it's the book you want. My employees are honest, hard working people with families who are counting on me to save their jobs. You know, not everyone is blessed with your talent, or the courage to live the way you do."

Cooper nodded in agreement. "I'm a lucky man, Joe. Very lucky," he said, smiling in reflection before his eyes narrowed with a question. "Have you thought about *how* you're going to pay them? I've enough to get by, but I don't have any funds to be advancing for that sort of thing. All I've got are my pictures."

Joe responded with a confident smile. "If Alicia is right, they're all we'll need."

Cooper settled back in the chair basking in the compliment. "Well, they say that everything has its time. I guess that's true, isn't it?"

"What do you mean, Dylan?" Alicia prompted.

"Oh, I've been meaning to take a picture of this bungalow for years; but I could never quite get around to it—not until the other day that is—and I've always wondered, why?" He struck a match on his pants and brought it to his pipe. "Now, I know."

"You've found this year's Christmas picture, haven't you?" Alicia prompted with a knowing smile.

"Aye," Cooper replied with a poignant sigh. "And perhaps much more."

PART TWO

Remember Christ our Savior,
Was born on Christmas Day . . .

Chapter Ten

The men who worked at Clements & Son were stunned by Joe's proposal. They stood around one of the layout tables in the middle of the shop, their eyes, along with their hopes, pinned on a man of ample girth wrapped in an ink-smeared printer's apron.

"In other words, Joe," Olaf Gundersen challenged in a voice that rang with disbelief and the graceful lilt of his Scandinavian ancestors, "You're asking us to work for no wages, aren't you?"

"No. No, Gundy, I'm not. What I said was—"

"Well, it bloody well sure sounds that way to me!" one of the linotype operators interrupted.

"To me too!" another bellowed, eliciting a chorus of angry rejoinders from the group.

"Hey! Hey, pipe down, now!" Gundersen scolded. An old world craftsman in his sixties, he was the acknowledged master here as well as father figure, general adviser, and foreman. "Let the man speak."

Joe thanked him with a nod and resumed. "I said that if we do a good job, if the book is a success and sells, we'll all get paid and our families'll have the kind of Christmas we want for them. If it doesn't, well . . ." He let it trail off and splayed his hands. "Then we're all back to where we are right now."

The men nodded in grudging agreement.

"So," Gundersen said, "there's still a chance we could do a lot of work without making a dime in the end. Right?"

"I'm afraid so," Joe replied. "It's risky. No doubt about it. I'm taking a chance, and I'm asking you to do the same."

Another disgruntled murmur rose from the group.

Cooper was standing in a distant corner of the shop with a portfolio tucked under his arm, and an ambivalent scowl on his face. On one hand, he'd known all along it was too good to be true, and was fighting an impulse to storm out of there. On the other, he was champing at the bit to come forward and let the pictures speak for themselves.

Joe caught his eye and signaled him to be patient, then fixed his gaze on his employees. "I understand how you all feel; but if you think it through, you'll realize you have everything to gain and nothing to lose. Unless—" A cacophony of protests erupted. Joe waited until the group settled down, then played his trump card. "I was about to say, unless you have other jobs lined up already. Is that the case?"

The fight went out of them, as Joe knew it would, and left a gloomy silence in its place. Most of the men just shrugged. A few shook their heads no. Others exchanged uncertain looks.

"Then that's your choice," Joe concluded. "Take a chance here, or take a chance out there."

Cooper raised a brow, clearly impressed by Joe's timing and canny reasoning.

Gundersen nodded and took the men aside. They huddled in animated discussion for a few moments until a consensus was reached, then drifted back toward Joe. "All right, Joseph," Gundersen challenged like a feisty schoolmaster. "You said you figure this book will be successful because people are going to buy it, that right?"

"That's right, Gundy."

"That means you're looking a bunch of your customers in the eye, right now," the rotund foreman concluded, gesturing to the workers behind him. "We figure the best way to make our decision is to have a look at those pictures."

"I was planning to show them to you," Joe replied, his voice ringing with confidence. He was about to wave Cooper over, but Cooper was already making his way between the huge machines. He charged into the middle of the group, placed the portfolio on the table and removed a neat stack of his Christmas pictures. He was still spacing them out when Joe's employees surged forward to examine them, buzzing with excitement.

Chapter Eleven

The photoengravers on Dorchester Street in East Boston had spent the week cutting plates from a sampling of Cooper's pictures; and Clements & Son's finest press, a Mergenthaler rotary gravure with automatic and single-sheet feed, had spent it being cleaned, oiled, and recalibrated to microscopic tolerances.

Now, Gundersen set the first plate into the bed and locked it in position. The apprentices usually adjusted the inking rollers and fine-tuned the platen, but the old master insisted on doing it himself this time. When satisfied all was in order, he double-checked the paper feeder, and thumbed the green bakelite start button that was labeled in German. The press hissed to life, and quickly settled into its five-beat syncopation, spewing out proofs.

Joe slipped one from the stack and carried it to a layout table where Cooper was waiting with the original—a stunning print of a young woman cradling an infant that he'd taken at the Boston North Station decades ago. The one that had come to be called Madonna and Child. "Not bad for a test run," Joe announced proudly, placing them side by side.

"No, not bad at all," Gundersen chimed in after shutting down the press.

They both searched Cooper's face for a reaction.

"Dylan?" Joe finally prompted.

Cooper had remained impassive. Now he scowled. "Not bad, Joe, *terrible*."

"Terrible?" Joe gasped.

"That's a hundred-twenty line screen," Gundersen protested.

"Gundy's right. It sure couldn't be any sharper."

"Aye, it's plenty sharp," Cooper conceded. "The trouble is, it's flat. No sparkle. See?" He stabbed a gnarled finger at the offending proof, then flicked it across the table toward Joe. "The blacks are weak. They don't have enough depth. No, it's just not good enough. It has to be darker, richer."

Joe's troubled eyes shifted back to his foreman. "Gundy?" he pleaded.

Gundersen hooked his thumbs behind the yoke of his apron and shook his head no. "Darker? You know as well as I, it's impossible without losing definition."

"Why?" Cooper challenged. He'd always been as uncompromising with others as he was with himself, and decided this was no time to change.

"Because the process has limitations," Joe replied, his voice taking on a bit of an edge. "If we force the plate to hold any more ink, the detail will block up, and the whites will start going gray." He looked to his foreman for confirmation, but Gundersen was deep in thought, and didn't notice.

"Well, we have to do something, Joe," Cooper exhorted, unwilling to accept it. "Because we sure aren't publishing them like this."

Joe's shoulders sagged in defeat. "Then I guess we aren't publishing them at all."

Cooper sighed with frustration.

"Excuse me, gentlemen," Gundersen said in an assertive tone. "I may have been a bit hasty before."

"Oh?" Joe prompted.

"Well, for what it's worth, it occured to me we might try running these like a two-color job."

"Two-color job?" Joe echoed, mystified. "I'm not sure I follow you, Gundy."

"Well, you're absolutely right when you say we can't put any more ink on the plate," Gundersen replied trying to be diplomatic. "But there's nothing that says we can't put more ink on the page."

Joe tilted his head in thought. "Yes, yes, that just might do it."

Cooper's eyes were darting back and forth between them. "Would you mind explaining what you two are going on about?"

"Instead of using two plates and two colors," Joe replied with growing enthusiasm. "We run the same plate and same color ink, twice, on the same page."

"Black on black," Cooper grunted, his face taking on a skeptical glower.

"The registration's got to be perfect, Gundy," Joe warned. "Think you can hold it?"

"Only one way to find out." Gundersen stepped to his press. Joe and the others gathered around him. Cooper folded his arms across his chest, and watched from a distance as Gundersen transferred the first run proofs to the paper-feed mechanism; then arranged them precisely, and started the press.

Joe took the first double-printed proof from the press and brightened. "It's better, Gundy; a lot better."

He handed it to Cooper. "Get your original, Dylan."

Cooper studied it briefly. "No need to, Joe. Look, it has life. It breathes." His book was suddenly a step closer to becoming a reality; and his heart pounded as he shook Gundersen's hand. "You're quite a genius, Gundy. Thanks."

Gundersen smiled with pride.

"Well," Joe said with relief, as he and Cooper walked to his office. "You can't ask for higher quality reproduction than that."

"Aye," Cooper replied with a preoccupied nod as they came through the door.

Joe sensed his distance. "Something wrong, Dylan?"

"No, not really," he replied evasively.

"Suit yourself; but your brow's got more furrows than a corn field. Has to be a reason for it."

"Well, it just dawned on me that Christmas is awful close, and, well . . ."

"True. We're going to be on a tight schedule. But I don't see any problem."

"I'm afraid I do, Joseph," Cooper said, fidgeting with his tobacco pouch. "I don't mean to rain on our parade, Joe; but I'm not sure I can make the rest of the prints in time."

Joe kicked back in his desk chair jauntily. "We'll just have to get you some help."

Cooper stiffened. "Help?" he echoed, displeased. "Oh, I don't know about that. I've always worked alone. Besides, I can't think of anyone who'd be—"

"I can," Joe interrupted, undaunted. "His name's Bartlett. Lucas Bartlett. He's young and talented, and has experience with halftone reproduction too."

"A photographer?"

"Uh-huh. I have some of his work right here. It wouldn't hurt to take a look. I think it's pretty good."

Cooper frowned. "I'll be the judge of that."

"Fair enough." Joe crossed to a filing cabinet and removed a manila envelope. It contained the shots of hand tools and farming equipment Bartlett had taken for Ed Mitchell's defunct hardware catalogue.

Cooper sorted through a few prints, then tossed the remainder onto Joe's desk. "Commercial work," he grunted, dismissing them.

"Well, sure. He's young and just starting out. A man has to earn a living."

"Indeed so, but I'm afraid it's just not my kind of photography, Joe."

"I'm well aware of that. Maybe, he's just never been exposed to it. This could be a chance for you to pass on your—"

"Legacy?" Cooper interrupted with a penetrating stare. "You weren't going to say that now, were you?"

Joe nodded with apprehension.

Cooper made no effort to soften the blow and scowled. "My pictures are my legacy, Joe."

"True, but all the great artists had apprentices—Michelangelo, da Vinci, Rembrandt—and I thought, maybe in the spirit of the season you might share some of your knowledge and experience with—"

"Enough, Joseph, enough," Cooper muttered with the pained expression of an adolescent being forced to do his chores. "You've more than made your point." He took several of Bartlett's prints from the desk and scrutinized them. "Well, technically they're quite sound. I imagine he'll do."

Chapter Twelve

Autumn's color had long faded and fallen, and the air in Cooper's darkroom had taken on a wintry chill. He and Bartlett had been literally living amid its soft red glow and pungent fumes. Prints were tacked on the walls, piled on every surface, and hung from drying racks. Test strips littered the floor. Empty cups and dishes with half eaten meals were scattered about in testimony to their single-mindedness.

Bartlett was standing at the long table bathed in crimson light. His hands, raw from constant contact with the chemicals, were gently rocking a print submerged in a tray of fixer.

Nearby, Cooper hunched over the printing table cleaning every last speck of dust from yet another eight-by-ten negative before sandwiching it beneath the cover glass with a sheet of photographic paper. When ready, he grasped the chain that hung from the bare bulb overhead, and squinted at Bartlett. "That one sufficiently fixed?"

Bartlett angled his watch to catch the red light. "Nope. Still about thirty seconds to go." The darkness concealed his smug expression, but not his tone, when he added, "There's a better way to do this, you know."

"Oh, is there now?" Cooper challenged, bristling at the remark.

"Sure is. For what it's worth, you wouldn't be waiting to

make that exposure, if we had a proper contact printer. It'd contain the light and you wouldn't have to worry about it fogging this—"

"Listen here, young man," Cooper interrupted, his burr rolling like angry thunder. "I've been doing it this way—my way—for fifty years; and I'm not about to be changing, now. Furthermore, speaking of worth—and it'd be a far sight from a king's ransom, mind you—your opinion would be best kept to yourself unless solicited." He scowled at the trays of chemicals on the table. "Besides, if you were tending to your business instead of mine, you'd have noticed we're low on developer, and already be mixing a fresh batch."

Bartlett scowled and began removing bottles of chemicals from the rack beneath the table. "Ought to be using ready-made, anyway," he said under his breath.

"Don't mumble, lad," Cooper prodded. "If you have something to say, say it."

Bartlett glanced at his watch. "I said you can make your exposure now."

Cooper grunted, and pulled the chain. The darkroom filled with blinding white light. He counted to ten and pulled it again, then removed the print from beneath the negative and glass, and slipped it into the tray of developer, hovering over it expectantly.

Several hours and countless prints later, cool rays of early morning light were streaming through the parlor windows as Cooper led the way from the darkroom, carrying a thick stack of prints.

"It's freezing in here," Bartlett said, his breath coming in little puffs between the words.

"That it is. I trust you can make a fire without burning the place to the ground?"

Bartlett nodded, shivering.

"Then get on with it, lad," Cooper bellowed in a feisty tone. "Or are you too tired?"

The young man stiffened with defiance. "Sounds to me like maybe the pot's calling the kettle black."

Cooper snorted with disdain, doing his best to conceal his shortness of breath. The years spent in fume-filled darkrooms had taken their toll, and Dr. Cheever had diagnosed him as consumptive.

They'd both been up all night, and neither would give the other the satisfaction of knowing he was exhausted; nor would Bartlett acknowledge that he was amazed by his elder's stamina. Bleary-eyed, he went to the woodbox and began tossing pieces of kindling and split logs into the fireplace.

Cooper began spacing the prints out in neat rows on the floor beneath the windows. They were all made from the same negative—a magnificent picture of the Newbury Community Church after a heavy snowfall—but they weren't the same at all. Indeed, there were differences of tone, contrast, and sharpness. Some that would be obvious to anyone, others that only Cooper could see. He knelt on the floor evaluating them, culling out those that were unacceptable until only two prints remained; then with the popping and creaking of aching joints, he struggled to his feet, and glanced to his assistant. "Come over 'ere, lad."

Bartlett had already put a match to the newspaper he'd stuffed beneath the andirons, and hungry flames were licking at the logs and soot-coated bricks that lined the fireplace. He rubbed his hands together, spreading the warmth, then joined Cooper at the window.

"You have a preference?" Cooper prompted, holding the prints side by side in the daylight.

"I may be wrong," Bartlett said with a facetious grin, "but I have a vague feeling you're soliciting my opinion?"

Cooper broke into a self-satisfied smile and nodded. "For what it's worth."

Bartlett studied the prints, his head tilting this way and that. "This one," Bartlett said decisively, indicating the one on the left.

"Really?" Cooper said in his intimidating way. "Did you play eenie meenie minie moe? Or do you actually have a reason?"

"I've a reason."

"Let's hear it then."

"Okay. I picked that one because it has a little more snap than the other."

"Snap, eh?"

Bartlett nodded, sensing he was in trouble.

"Aye, that it does; but you see, lad, that much contrast doesn't suit the nature of the picture, now does it?" Cooper punctuated the remark with a crisp nod; and without waiting for a reply, tossed the print Bartlett had selected to the floor with the other discards. "Better gather those up."

Bartlett knew Cooper was right but was loath to admit it. He waited until his back was turned, then took a half-hearted swipe at the prints with his foot, and went about collecting them.

Cooper bent to the packing crate that he used as a coffee table, and placed the chosen print in a box with others that had survived the culling-out process. A smile of weary satisfaction spread across his face as he closed the lid.

"What do you want to do with these?" Bartlett asked, scooping up the last of the discards.

"Give them here, lad." Cooper snatched the prints from Bartlett, crossed to the fireplace, and without hesitation, tossed them into the roaring blaze.

Bartlett winced. Despite the subtle differences, he thought

that each print had artistic merit if taken on its own, and was shocked by Cooper's indifference.

Cooper broke into a knowing smile as the prints curled and burst into flame. "Good work, Lucas," he said, his face aglow in the flickering light. "That's a fine fire."

Chapter Thirteen

Cooper's truck turned into Sycamore Street, sending leaves swirling across the pavement, and parked in front of the printing shop. He got out and hurried inside with the box of photographs, greeting the workmen as he made his way between the noisy equipment to Joe's office.

Prints of his Christmas pictures covered the walls now. A layout table, where Alicia sat blocking out the pages for the book, ran the length of the glass partition. Joe was directly opposite her at his desk, the phone pressed to his ear. He seemed tethered to it as of late, taking orders from the many buyers, shopkeepers, and book distributors to whom he'd sent samples of Cooper's photographs.

"That's right, Mr. Hastings," he said smartly. "We'll guarantee delivery in time—I know it's tight, but the book's worth waiting for, and you know it—Fine. We won't let you down—Do our best, Mr. Hastings. With luck, we might even get them to you sooner—Sure, I have that information right here." He swiveled to a bookcase, fetched a binder, and began flipping through the pages, nodding to Cooper who trudged into the office.

Alicia looked up from her work and brightened as he handed her the box. "Well, good morning."

"You said it. That's the last of 'em."

Alicia removed the prints, and began shuffling through them with growing anticipation. "They're beautiful, Dylan. Beautiful," she exclaimed, her eyes widening with delight. "Every one of them."

Cooper beamed, and settled his weary body into a chair. "Thank you. I was up the entire weekend printing them."

"The entire weekend?" she echoed puzzled. "What about Lucas? I thought he was helping?"

Cooper grinned wryly and waggled a hand. "Well, as we say in Scotland, 'More than one cook to a haggis, is one cook to a haggis too many.'"

Alicia laughed and returned her attention to the photographs. She was nearing the last few when she paused at a landscape. The rhythmic composition of rolling countryside, dark winter sky, and road lined by bare, perfectly aligned trees was breathtaking; but it was the young woman in the foreground that caught Alicia's eye. Bathed in delicate crosslight that made her dress appear to be illuminated from within, she had a tranquil beauty about her and held herself with the balanced poise of a dancer.

Alicia held the print up to Cooper. "That's the road that goes by your cottage, isn't it?"

"Uh-huh. Years ago. Before they paved it."

"And what about her? Who's she?"

"Oh, just a girl."

"The one you were sweet on?" Alicia prompted coyly.

Cooper emitted a nervous chuckle. "No, she just happened to be walking by one day, and I just happened to be there with my camera, that's all."

"Like the morning you were photographing our bungalow and I came out to say hello?"

"Rather like that."

"Just another Christmas picture, hmmm?"

"I didn't say that," Cooper chided. "And if it will spare me further interrogation, the fact of the matter is, it's not really a Christmas picture—I've included it because it's—it's—a picture of—" He noticed Joe had just hung up the phone and promptly changed the subject. "Joe? Joe, I think that grin you're wearing means we ought to be listening to what you've got to say."

Joe smiled, letting the suspense build as he pushed back from the desk and joined them. "We just got another order. Hastings and Brown, they're one of the biggest wholesalers in Boston."

"Good work, lad!" Cooper bellowed, getting to his feet to shake Joe's hand.

Alicia let out a whoop, wrapped one arm around Joe, the other around Cooper, and pulled them as close as her pregnant tummy would allow.

Chapter Fourteen

Several weeks had passed, and on this chilly autumn morning in Newbury, a large forest green van was parked amidst the colorful leaves outside the printing shop. Fanciful gold lettering on the side proclaimed Agostini's Bindery.

Inside, where the presses were going full tilt, a wiry man with Mediterranean features and a flowing mustache stood in animated conversation with Gundersen.

Joe was at his desk reassuring another prospective buyer that they could deliver Cooper's book in time when Gundersen stuck his head into the office. "Joe? Joe, see you for a minute?"

"Sure," Joe replied, concerned by his foreman's tone. "You have a problem?"

"In a manner of speaking," Gundersen replied unhappily. "Actually, Mr. Agostini does."

Joe was leading the way from the office when Mr. Agostini came charging toward them. "Look, Mister Clements," he said, raising his voice over the racket. "We can do anything; anything within reason; but, as I've explained to your foreman—"

"Of course you can," Joe interrupted. "That's why we came to you."

"Ah, yes, well," Agostini sputtered, momentarily confounded. "I was about to say, you want quality binding, and you want it fast, and you want it cheap. Now, something has to give."

"Well, Mr. Agostini," Joe said, sounding perplexed. "I'm

running out of time—and I have a tight budget, which leaves—" he paused for effect and splayed his hands before concluding "—dare I say, quality?"

Agostini's moustache twitched as if electrified.

"Of course," Joe went on before Agostini could interject. "I'd be very disappointed if you were forced to lower your standards, and produce a—"

Agostini flared at the insult. "Hold on right there, Mr. Clements. Forty-five years I build this business. Forty-five years I work hard and make a reputation. Forty-five years I sweat and—" Agostini paused suddenly, realizing that Joe had shrewdly cornered him, and nodded in resignation. "Okay, when do I get the rest of the pages?"

"Gundy?" Joe prompted, his brow arched with apprehension.

"End of the week," Gundersen replied.

Agostini groaned in dismay. "Tomorrow is already too late. I do my best. Remember, I make no promises."

Joe smiled, feeling a bit more confident. "I'll remember, Mr. Agostini." They shook hands, and Agostini hurried off between the thundering presses.

Indeed, in the weeks that followed, the shop vibrated day and night with their catchy syncopation, augmented by the crisp whisk of the paper cutter, the supportive chatter among the workers, and the growing sense that something special was happening here. Soon, everyone had become imbued with the Christmas spirit. Alicia hung a large wreath with a bright red bow and clusters of pine cones and berries in the front window, and spent the day decorating the shop with sprigs of holly and magnificent poinsettias from her garden.

Then, all of a sudden, the last plate was locked in the Mergenthaler's bed, the last of the photographs printed, the last pages trimmed and sent to the bindery, the last orders filled, and the last truck loaded. Gundersen and the workers joined Joe,

Alicia, and Cooper on the loading dock to see it off. They cheered and waved as the truck pulled away, leaving them with a euphoric sense of satisfaction.

"You know, I never dreamed we'd get so many orders," Alicia said brightly.

"We wouldn't have gotten any if it wasn't for you," Joe said, gazing at her with affection and pride.

"I've a feeling this is going to be the best Christmas we've ever had!" Gundersen exclaimed.

"Let's not get over confident," Joe cautioned.

"That usually means trouble," Gundersen prompted.

"I wouldn't say trouble, Gundy, but there's still the possibility that people won't buy the book."

"So?" one of the workers challenged. "That's not our problem, is it?"

"I'm afraid so," Joe replied, squirming like a worm on a hook. "You see, books are bought by retailers on consignment. That means every one they don't sell can be sent back to the publisher. That's how the business works."

"Hold on there," another piped up. "We've never had anything sent back before."

"Because we've never been the publisher before."

"And they get their bloody money back?" a third asked, his voice ringing with disbelief.

Joe responded with a sheepish nod.

"You should have said something when you first came to us, Joe," Gundersen protested.

"I would have, Gundy, believe me. But I've been learning as I go. I didn't know at the time. Would it have mattered?"

The workers exchanged looks then, realizing they'd still have had little choice, began shrugging and shaking their heads no. "I suppose not," Gundersen finally said. "Nothing we can do now, anyway."

"Well, there is one thing," Alicia said, her voice taking on a reverent timbre as she glanced at Joe. "We can all start praying that people buy them."

Joe frowned. "Pray? I'm not sure that would do any good."

"Pray all you like, lass," Cooper chimed in, "but take my word for it, people will be buying them, regardless."

"You sound awfully sure of that, Dylan," Alicia observed. "Have you a special reason why?"

"My Christmas pictures," the old fellow replied proudly. "Or have you all forgotten they're what sold you on doing this in the first place?"

Chapter Fifteen

The apprehensive silence that descended on the printing shop turned everyone's attention outward, to the other stores and shops that lined Newbury's bare-treed streets. And soon, despite hard times and the pressures to make ends meet, the village came alive with the sparkle of Christmas decorations, the scent of ginger and rum-laced fruit from the bakery, and the energetic cacophony of holiday activity: The cheery salutations of street corner Santas; the clatter of vehicles hurrying home with freshly cut evergreens lashed to their roofs; the squeals and laughter of children; the spirited voices of carolers; and the heartening ring of cash registers.

Alicia spent the time writing Christmas cards and shopping for simple gifts; and Joe spent it pacing in his office, worrying that they couldn't afford them; but just as the weeks of tension and suspense were threatening to overwhelm him, the pin-drop quiet that had fallen over the shop was suddenly broken. Not by the rumble of trucks returning cartons of unsold books as they had all feared, but by the ringing phone in Joe's office, and by the anxious voices of sales clerks, buyers, and distributors who had sold their last book and were calling to order more copies. One call was especially encouraging and sent Joe hurrying into the shop to announce, "Hastings and Brown just doubled their order!"

He returned to his desk and was happily tallying sales figures when it dawned on him that this was like the first pump of oil out of a new well. He spent the next several hours looking for a way to keep it coming. The idea that finally struck him was far too ambitious to undertake on his own, so he called Arthur Hastings back and asked if he'd come to Newbury to discuss it. He decided not to mention it to anyone—not even to Alicia—until he was certain he had the canny businessman's support.

In the meantime, the flood of orders continued, setting off a wave of activity and excitement that kept the presses going, and finally crested with the promise of snow and the peal of church bells. They reverberated throughout every home and touched every heart, and had special meaning for those gathered at Clements & Son on Sycamore Street.

Christmas was barely a week away and all of Joe's employees, their wives and children, along with Alicia, Cooper, Bartlett, and Mr. Agostini, had come together to celebrate the book's success.

The atmosphere in the gaily decorated shop, where clusters of red candles flickered, was one of satisfaction and quiet reflection at first; then, thanks to the plates of homemade Christmas cookies and a kettle of steaming mulled wine, it became more jovial and alive—especially when Gundersen came bursting in dressed up as Santa Claus and began passing out candy canes to the children who, one by one, sat on his knee, telling Santa what they wanted for Christmas.

Alicia fetched a box camera and began taking pictures of them, and Joe, like his father before him, began passing out thick pay envelopes and Christmas bonuses to their parents.

When they'd finished, Alicia produced a beautifully wrapped package and handed it to Cooper. "Merry Christmas, Dylan!"

"And what might that be?" Cooper wondered, eyes widening with intrigue as everyone gathered around him.

"Open it and find out," Alicia prompted.

"Yes—Come on—Open it," a chorus of anxious voices shouted, joining in.

Cooper tore at the wrapping and removed a copy of his book that had been bound in leather. The cover was inscribed in gold leaf which proclaimed: *The Christmas Pictures*, Photographs by Dylan Cooper. The old fellow's eyes glistened with emotion. "Well, I . . . I don't know what to say. Thank you. Thank you all for everything." He ran his fingers over the binding, impressed with the craftsmanship. "It's a fine job."

"Mr. Agostini did it for us," Joe explained. "It's just about the only copy we didn't sell."

"Well, that calls for a toast," Cooper growled with a wink to the proud bookbinder as he raised his mug of wine. "Merry Christmas everyone!"

"Merry Christmas, Dylan!" everyone shouted in response. They were all remarking there hadn't been a better one in years when Joe fetched Alicia's camera and aimed it at Cooper.

The old fellow held up a hand in protest. Others did the posing, not he. "Oh, Joe, no. None of that, now. Come on, Joseph. Joseph."

"Oh, let him, Dylan," Alicia pleaded. "I'd like to have one. Please?"

Cooper stood there, awkwardly, not sure what to do with his hands. Finally, he jammed one into a pocket and made the other into a fist that he set against a hip. "All right," he growled, satisfied with his defiant pose. "Let's be done with it."

"Come on, a big smile now," Alicia said brightly.

Cooper's jaw tightened further, then, an instant before the shutter clicked, he relented and allowed an impish grin to break across his face.

Alicia smiled with amusement. Pure, unabridged Dylan Cooper, she thought as Joe embraced her, their eyes glistening with joy, and the knowledge that next Christmas there'd be another member of the family to share their happiness. "As Pastor Martin would say, all is going according to Plan, isn't it, darling?"

"Yeah, I guess so," Joe replied as everyone broke into song.

"God rest ye merry gentlemen,
Let nothing you dismay . . .
Remember Christ our Savior,
Was born on Christmas day . . ."

Alicia and Joe joined in the spirited singing that brought the party to a rousing conclusion. Later, after everyone had left, the two of them embraced, savoring their good fortune, then went about cleaning up the shop. Alicia was humming the carol and reflecting on its lyrics as she cleared the worktables when something occurred to her. "You know, I think sometimes we forget the true meaning of Christmas."

"Maybe. But not today," Joe said with evident pride. "I've never seen so many happy faces."

"Yes, it was very special," Alicia said, deciding on a subtle approach to an idea she'd been entertaining. "Tomorrow is the Sunday before Christmas, isn't it?"

"Uh-huh, I believe so. Why?"

"Well, I may be wrong," she replied, pretending she couldn't remember, "but I vaguely recall that if Christmas doesn't fall on a Sunday, that's when the children put on the annual Christmas play, isn't it?"

"Yeah, I guess," Joe replied, sweeping bits of party debris into a corner. "The only thing I remember about the Christmas play is that I was always a shepherd, never a wise man."

"Well, there's hope for you yet."

Joe responded with a good-natured chuckle. "Of course, you were always the Blessed Virgin."

"Not anymore," Alicia said with an alluring giggle, before blithely adding, "By the way, Pastor Martin said it's at evening services this year. I think we should go."

Joe stopped his broom in midstroke and looked over at her. "You mean to church?"

"Yes, Joe, to church," Alicia replied, unable to suppress a little smile at his reaction. "We have a lot to be thankful for, and . . ."

"True," Joe groaned, sensing the inevitable. "I can't argue with that, but—"

". . . and it'd be the perfect opportunity to ask God's blessing on the blessed event, too."

"Yes, I guess it would . . ."

"Does that mean you're coming with us?" Alicia prompted, brightly, cradling her tummy.

Joe smiled in capitulation. "Sure, why not, if it'll make you happy."

Alicia's eyes widened with delight. "Happy? Oh, Joe, it would be the best Christmas present ever."

Chapter Sixteen

The next evening, the Town Square was crowded with vehicles and alive with people streaming toward the Newbury Community Church from every street and corner. Aglow with light and bedecked with colorful Christmas decor, the white-steepled structure resonated with the soaring voices of the choir as Joe and Alicia joined the other members of the congregation who filled every pew to capacity.

A large creche that served as the setting for the Christmas play stood on one side of the altar. Two school children dressed as Mary and Joseph knelt at the hay-filled manger where a figure of the infant Jesus lay. As church bells rang, a procession of children in homemade costumes came down the aisle to the altar and encircled the creche.

As the choir reached its final crescendo, Pastor Martin, resplendent in the white alb and red sash he wore for holiday services, stepped to the pulpit. "In these troubled times, with Europe once again, beset by war, it is especially fitting that I welcome you to our annual Christmas play that celebrates the birth of our Lord Jesus Christ, the Prince of Peace." He paused and gestured to the nativity scene. "It takes place on the night when the wise men, having journeyed from the East, arrived at the stable in Bethlehem to worship the newborn Messiah."

Pastor Martin paused again as three children, dressed as wise men, came forward carrying gifts. They knelt at the manger, heads bowed in tribute to the Christ child.

"Though there is no specific number in the scriptures," Pastor Martin resumed, "we assume there were three 'magi' because the Bible mentions three different gifts that were offered to the Lord.

"The second chapter of Matthew tells us these wise men had been guided by His star." The pastor's eyes drifted to a shimmering tinfoil star suspended above the creche. "No doubt they were aware of Numbers, chapter 24, verse 17, which records that . . . ." He paused and nodded in the direction of the children.

". . . 'A Star shall come out of Jacob, and a Scepter shall rise out of Israel'," a girl of eight recited, barely able to contain her excitement.

"What exactly was this star that guided them to Bethelem?" Pastor Martin resumed. "Some believe it was a natural phenomenon caused by the simultaneous aligning of Mars, Jupiter, and Saturn. Others believe it was a supernatural phenomenon similar to the 'pillar of fire' witnessed by many in the Old Testament.

"Though we aren't certain which phenomena the wise men observed, many biblical scholars believe they were descended from a group of astronomers in the sixth century BC who were taught by the prophet Daniel how to recognize the birth of Christ.

"In Matthew, chapter 2, verses 9 and 10, we're told that . . ." Pastor Martin let it tail off and nodded to the children again.

". . . that . . . that the Star the wise men had seen 'went before them and stood over . . . stood over where the young Child was'," one of the children responded, beset by a mild case of stage fright. "'When they saw the star, they rejoiced with exceedingly great joy'."

"And why were the wise men so filled with joy?" Pastor

Martin asked with a rhetorical pause. "Because they knew that the hundreds of prophecies concerning the coming Messiah were finally coming true!" he concluded, his voice rising with fervor. "As the angel announced to the shepherds in the field . . ."

". . . 'For there is born to you this day in the City of David a Savior who is Christ the Lord'," a girl wearing an angel costume with floppy wings said.

"And as an angel speaking to Joseph said of his wife Mary . . ." Pastor Martin went on with another pause.

". . . 'She will bring forth a son, and you shall call His name Jesus,'" another of the children replied, his voice cracking with adolescent charm. "'For He will save His people from their sins.'"

"To save His people," Pastor Martin repeated. "That was His whole reason for coming, wasn't it? To give His life in atonement for the sins of the world. That's the true meaning of Christmas."

Joe couldn't help but recall Alicia's comment the day before about the true meaning of Christmas being forgotten; though, he didn't think Alicia had Pastor Martin's meaning in mind. On the contrary, far from seeing them as sinners in need of redemption, Joe was certain that, like him, Alicia thought of them as decent people who cared deeply for their fellow man, and had done well on behalf of those who were dependent on them.

"And because of Christ's death on the cross," Pastor Martin went on, "you can have forgiveness of sins here tonight by accepting the sacrifice He made on your behalf, and by inviting Him into your heart. If any of you would like to have your sins forgiven by the Lord and receive the gift of eternal life, please come forward," the Pastor concluded, signaling the choir with a wave of his hand.

As the church once again filled with soaring voices, more than a dozen members of the congregation stood and slipped from their pews. The town's mayor, Dr. Cheever, and Olaf Gundersen, the foreman in Joe's shop, were among those who walked down the aisle and knelt at the manger that held the Christ child.

Alicia stole an anxious glance at Joe, hoping he would join them; but Joe remained seated in the pew, unmoved by the pastor's invitation.

A short time later, they were driving home along the coast road when Joe sensed Alicia wasn't sitting close to him as she usually did, but far across the seat, her gaze fixed out the side window. "Alicia?"

"Uh-huh?"

"Are you okay?"

"I'm fine."

"You're sure? Nothing starting to happen with the baby or anything?"

"Nope, too early."

"Good. By the way, just in case you're wondering," Joe said with a hint of sarcasm, "I asked because you haven't said a word since we left the church. Now I'm getting the silent treatment. What's going on?"

Alicia pursed her lips, making a decision. "Well, I guess I'm a little disappointed you didn't respond to Pastor Martin's invitation to come forward and—"

"Stop right there, young lady," Joe commanded, guiding the roadster through a curve. "You said my coming along this evening would be the best Christmas gift ever, didn't you?"

"Yes, I did, but—"

"But what? You just said it to make sure I—"

"No. No, it's just that I was hoping you'd—"

"You know how you sound, Alicia? Like a child who gets a new bicycle for Christmas and complains it doesn't have a bell on the handlebar."

Alicia sighed in contrition. "You're right. I'm sorry. It's just that, despite our good fortune, these are still uncertain times; and I thought, maybe as . . . as Pastor Martin said . . . inviting Christ into your heart might help you cope with them."

"You're right," Joe said in a tone that belied his words. "The business barely survived; and I have serious concerns about the future. But I didn't ask for God's help—then—or now. I went to church tonight because I thought it would make you happy, remember?"

"Oh, Joseph, of course I do; and it did; but I want *you* to be happy, too. I hate to see you worrying about your workers . . . about making ends meet . . . about—"

"I *am* happy," Joe protested. He swung the roadster into the driveway and parked behind the bungalow, then turned to Alicia. "You want to know what's really going to make me happy?"

Alicia nodded, expecting it had something to do with her, and brightened in anticipation.

". . . If this meeting I'm having with Mr. Hastings tomorrow goes well."

Alicia looked surprised. "Mr. Hastings? You didn't say anything about a meeting."

Joe winced, wishing he hadn't said it. "I didn't want to get your hopes up. No questions, okay? I don't want to hear another word about it."

Alicia nodded, then smiled at what she was about to say. "I'll pray in silence, I promise."

Chapter Seventeen

A light snow was dusting the rugged landscape as the train from Boston wound through the foothills and thundered into Newbury Station, clouds of steam hissing from its wheel-housings.

Arthur Hastings, an angular man in a heavy winter coat, stepped from the coach, carrying an impressive briefcase, and strode to the taxi stand.

Clements & Son was shut down for the holidays, but Joe had been waiting in his office for over an hour when Hastings arrived. "Mr. Hastings," he said brightly, getting to his feet to greet him.

"Arthur, please," Hastings said extending a hand. "This has turned out to be quite a holiday season, hasn't it?"

"Thanks to all those books you ordered. More than anyone else, according to my records."

"I'm not surprised. The response from my outlets has been nothing short of amazing," Hastings said, the planes of his face animating along with his tone. "Needless to say, I'm more than curious about this idea you mentioned. What kind of book do you have in mind?"

"Not a book, Arthur," Joe replied, his voice rising in excitement. "A *series* of books. Each one will feature something special about the New England area: the people, the industries, the landscape, the sea coast, the rivers and streams, and so on."

Hastings's eyes widened with interest. "Good idea, Joe. Very good, but . . ." He let it tail off, then nodded toward the shop. ". . . It doesn't look to me like you're set up to handle it."

"Nothing that buying a couple of presses and putting on some more people wouldn't cure."

Hastings broke into a knowing smile. "That's where I come in, isn't it?"

"Exactly. Things have been looking up as of late, but I'm still in no position to finance the operation. I was hoping you'd see the potential and—"

"I'd have to be a fool not to," Hastings enthused. "I'm sure we can work out a financial arrangement that would be satisfactory to both of us."

"I've no doubt of it, Arthur."

"Good. There is one condition, though," Hastings said with a suspenseful pause. "Cooper has to take the pictures. He has a reverence for this area, Joe. An intimacy with it that gives his pictures a certain—" he paused, searching for a word that eluded him—"a certain nostalgic quality. That's what sold his Christmas pictures, and that's what'll sell these."

"I couldn't agree more."

"But you haven't approached Cooper with the idea yet, have you?"

"No, I wanted to talk to you first. Why?"

"Well, I've heard rumors he's an independent old bird who won't take on a commercial assignment."

"They're not rumors," Joe said with an affectionate chuckle.

"Not surprising. Of all my European suppliers, the Scotsmen, despite their canny knack for business, are the most stubborn and set in their ways."

"Dylan can be stubborn; but if you're his friend, if he trusts you . . . Well, that's another matter."

Hastings nodded sagely, then stood and shook Joe's hand. "I'll be waiting to hear from you. Merry Christmas."

"Merry Christmas to you, Arthur."

The meeting left Joe's heart pounding with hope and apprehension. He leaned back in his chair and stared out the window at the falling snow, thinking about how and when he'd broach the subject with Cooper.

Chapter Eighteen

The storm continued throughout the day and most of the next; and as Christmas Eve descended upon Newbury, the bungalow nestled amidst drifts of wind-driven snow. It dotted every thicket and coated every tree, and crunched beneath the tires of Cooper's truck that cut graceful tracks in the thick blanket on the shoreline road.

Inside the cab, Cooper and Joe sat side by side singing England's Carol at the top of their lungs to the rhythmic slap of the wipers; and when they reached the bungalow, their exuberant voices brought Alicia to the door just in time to see them hoisting a Christmas tree from the truck's bed. The magnificent spruce filled the parlor with its rich aroma and, when secured in its stand, came to within a foot of the peaked ceiling.

After dinner, Alicia went to the fireplace and hung three stockings from the mantel with thumb tacks. She crossed her arms above her bulging tummy, and smiled at the tiny stocking on the end before joining Joe and Dylan who were trimming the tree with lights, ornaments and shimmering tinsel.

"That's the nicest tree we've ever had, isn't it?" Alica enthused.

"It certainly is," Joe replied, stepping back to admire it. He had just placed an illuminated star atop the tree, and the mirrored facets sent shafts of light dancing across the ceiling.

Cooper looked almost misty-eyed. "Can't remember the last

time I had one," he whispered; then struck by a thought, he exclaimed, "Oh, I almost forgot!" He hurried outside to his truck and, moments later, returned with a faded Christmas box that he had tied with new ribbon. "Merry Christmas," he said, handing it to Alicia. "You might want to open it now."

Alicia settled on the floor next to the tree, then undid the bow with childlike enthusiasm and lifted the top. Within the folds of tissue, she found a small wooden stable, along with figures of Joseph, Mary, the Three Wise Men, a manger that held the Christ child, and an angel with a flowing sash that proclaimed: Gloria In Excelsis Deo. Sculpted of fired-clay, they were all of exquisite proportion and detail. "Oh, Dylan, they're so beautiful," Alicia exclaimed as she continued unwrapping them. "Where did you get them?"

Cooper had settled in one of the wicker chairs with a brandy and his pipe, and was staring at the crackling Christmas Eve fire, lost in his thoughts.

"Dylan?"

"Oh, sorry," he said, coming out of it.

"I was wondering where you got these," Alicia prompted, handing one of the figures to Joe.

"From the bottom of a closet," Cooper replied with an impish grin.

Alicia looked skeptical. "A closet?"

"Aye, they were a gift. Christmas . . . nineteen-eighteen; but I was away at war, so they were set aside, or so I imagine. Years later, I was cleaning out some closets, and there was the box beneath a pile of junk with a lovely Christmas card affixed to it."

"Well, whoever gave them to you had a fine eye," Joe observed, appreciating the figure's graceful gesture.

"Aye, that she did . . ."

"She?" Alicia echoed with a knowing smile. "The girl in the photograph," she declared.

"Aye, the girl in the photograph," Cooper finally conceded

with a poignant sigh. "Her name was Grace. Grace MacVicar." He rolled the r's, clearly savoring the sound of them.

"Something tells me she was from Scotland too," Alicia prompted.

"Aye. A dancer she was. Classically trained. Her ballet troupe performed the world over." He paused and drew thoughtfully on his pipe, deciding whether or not he'd share the rest with them. "She was my soul mate, and I hers. Right from the beginning it was as if our hearts beat as one. We'd been married for just three days when I went off to war. A few months later Grace wrote that she was pregnant. As you might imagine, I was overcome with joy and couldn't wait to get home to be with her and the baby." He set the pipe aside and took a long sip of brandy. ". . . but I didn't get there in time. The baby came early . . . too early. Didn't live for more than a couple of hours."

"Oh, Dylan, no," Alicia said, her voice ringing with empathy.

A veil of sadness clouded Cooper's eyes. "Such is life, I'm afraid. Things might've been different if I'd been with her . . ." He took a long swallow of brandy then shook his head at the tragic irony of what he was about to say. "As it turned out, Grace was still suffering from the loss when the Army sent a telegram sayin' I'd been killed in action."

"Oh, dear," Alicia groaned, her hand tightening around the figure from the creche she'd been holding. "What a horrible mistake."

"Aye, as horrible as they come; but not uncommon in the chaos of war. After that, well, Grace just wasn't the same. By the time I got home, she'd already gone back to Scotland to be with her family." Cooper took another swallow of brandy, then another, draining the glass. "My tongue gets any looser, I'll start talking about the time I went home to find her."

"Did you?" Alicia wondered.

"No. No, Alicia, I didn't," Cooper replied with a wistful sigh. "You see, her family never approved of her life on the stage, and when she appeared on their doorstep, they vowed she'd never leave again, and—" Alicia interrupted in disbelief. "Because she was a dancer?"

"Aye, they weren't much for the arts," Cooper replied with a sarcastic scowl. "Her father was a . . .a . . . well, I was about to say, a meanspirited fool, but since it's Christmas, let's just say he was a rather provincial chap, who looked me square in the eye and insisted that Grace's misfortune was fair and just punishment for her wantonness. I could hardly believe what I was hearing; and when I took exception to it, the man had the nerve to say that she'd have come to see the error of her ways and become the dutiful daughter had she not married me."

"He—he—he blamed you for what happened?" Alicia sputtered in disbelief.

"Aye, along with her brother who was entrusted with protecting her virtue," Cooper replied with an angry snort. "You'd think I was the devil himself. Her father not only accused me of destroying her, but vowed I'd never have an opportunity to do so again."

"But you were away at war, and—and Grace thought you'd been killed. How could he—"

Cooper nodded emphatically. "And he let her go on thinking it—to this day as far as I know."

"In other words," Joe concluded, "Grace's family wouldn't tell her you were alive; and wouldn't tell you—wouldn't tell her husband—where to find her?"

"Not only that, they did whatever they could to stop me. Even threatened her brother with disownment if he revealed her whereabouts or told her I'd survived the war." Cooper paused and looked off in reflection. "Not a bad fellow, Colin. He cared deeply for his sister, just didn't have her backbone. I looked for her anyway; traveled to more towns and villages . . . made inquiries at post offices, churches, and hospitals . . . all to no avail, of course. That's where I'm from too, by the way, Dumbarton. It's just outside of Glasgow. Rugged coastal terrain, hearty people."

"Sounds familiar," Joe observed.

"Aye, much like New England in many ways," Cooper replied with a reflective smile. "But maybe—maybe I'll get back to Scotland just once more. You never know . . ." He then came out of the reverie and pushed up from the chair, unsteadily. "Enough of that now. Where's my jacket?"

"Not so fast. We haven't opened our presents yet," Joe said, guiding him back to the chair. "There's a special one for you."

Cooper looked surprised. "For me? I already have my present, Joe."

"Well, it's for both of you," Joe explained with a wink to Alicia who looked as surprised as Cooper. "We're going to be publishing another book. Actually a whole series of them."

"Joe . . ." Alicia admonished, a hint of fatigue creeping into her voice. "Something tells me your meeting went well."

Joe nodded emphatically. "Couldn't have gone better. The best part is . . ." Joe let it trail off as he uncorked the bottle of brandy and refilled Cooper's glass. "Our favorite photographer here is part of it."

Cooper forced a smile. "Am I now?"

"That's right," Joe replied. "A big part."

"Well," Alicia said, getting to her feet. "I'm afraid mother and 'son' are going to have to wait until morning to see what else Santa brought them. Aren't we? Yes. Yes, we are," she cooed, cradling her tummy in her arms. "I'm really pooped. I think I'll head off to bed. Okay?"

Joe nodded. "Of course, you 'both' need your rest. Merry Christmas."

"Merry Christmas, darling. You too, Dylan."

"Aye," Cooper replied, with a halfhearted smile as Alicia kissed his cheek, and left.

Joe waited until he heard the bedroom door close then turned to Cooper. "You know, it's hard to believe we almost went under."

"Joe," Cooper said with apprehension. "Joe, I hope—"

"This is really going to put us over the top," Joe went on. "It'll keep us going for years."

Cooper responded with an indulgent nod. "I hope you haven't committed me to anything."

"Of course not," Joe admonished. "Now, let's see if I can bring a smile to that sad old face?"

"Doubt it," Cooper grunted.

"You remember that fellow Hastings?" Joe began.

Cooper struck a match and brought it to his pipe. "Named a famous battle after him, didn't they?" he replied, pretending he couldn't recall.

"He sold more of your books than anyone else, and you know it."

Dylan nodded and exhaled a stream of pipe smoke. "Aye, it seems to ring a bell now."

"Well, he's going to finance us."

Dylan took a long swallow of brandy. "Finance us . . ."

"Uh-huh. Of course, we want all the pictures to be just like your book. Your—"

"Joe," Cooper interrupted.

"—Your style, your way of seeing things," Joe pressed on. "We want you to—"

"Joe? Joe, listen to me for a minute, will you?" Cooper interrupted, his tone sharpening. "There aren't going to be any more books. Not even one."

Joe took a moment to gather his thoughts. Then, sounding apologetic and somewhat hurt, he said, "Well, to be honest, I thought you might say that. I know you don't like taking on assignments. But we're friends, and I thought that might count for something. I wouldn't suggest you get involved, if I didn't think you'd enjoy it."

"I don't doubt that for a minute, Joe."

"Then, why not hear me out?"

"Because I have my book, Joe. I've no interest in another."

"But you'd have all the artistic freedom you'd require. And you could—"

Cooper shook his head no, emphatically.

"Why?" Joe challenged, his voice taking on a slight edge. "I mean, what are you afraid of?"

Cooper's eyes widened. "I'm not afraid, Joe. I'm just not interested." He rapped his pipe loudly against the side of an ashtray.

"You're serious, aren't you?"

Cooper rapped the pipe several more times in reply, knocking some smoldering ashes from the bowl. "Just like always, no is no." He jammed the pipe stem hard into the corner of his mouth and got to his feet.

"Well, no may be no; but no doesn't make sense, Dylan. This could bring you recognition. Even fame."

Cooper's brow knitted with frustration. "They're of no interest to me, Joe. I have what I want." He looked about, then pointed to a copy of his book on the table. "And I have you and Alicia to thank for it." His voice broke with emotion and he paused before adding, "I'll be forever grateful, Joe, believe me."

"No, no, Dylan, I'm the one who's grateful. I just wish you'd let me show it. You've worked so hard all these years. How can you turn your back on the rewards?"

"But I haven't, Joseph. I've always been my own man, and that's been my reward."

"Look," Joe snapped, losing patience with Cooper's obstinacy. "A lot of people worked on your book; and for some of us, the rewards are just beginning. You can't say no, just like that. It isn't fair."

Cooper took a deep breath, trying to maintain his composure. "But I can, Joseph; and I have. Now, why don't you just calm down, and—"

"Calm down?!" Joe exploded, his voice rising in half-octaves as he continued. "This may not mean much to you, but it's a once in a lifetime opportunity to me. The best chance I've ever had at getting some financial security."

"Well, go right ahead and take it!" Cooper shouted matching his volume. "Just stop lecturing me like I'm standing in your way. Like I'm the one who's keeping you from—" Cooper paused, struck by the implication of his own words. "Ah, now we're getting to work on the crust of the bread, aren't we, Joe?"

Joe winced in discomfort.

"All this talk about fame and recognition," Cooper went on, his burr thickening, his eyes taking on a feisty sparkle. "You can't hide mold with marmalade, Joe. What you're really saying is, I'm the key to you getting the financing. That's it. Isn't it?"

"So what if it is?" Joe replied, angry at being caught. "You have any idea how much money we could—"

"I don't care about money!" Cooper retorted.

"Well, I do!"

"Fine. You've every right to make as much as you can. But you'll have to do it without Dylan Cooper!"

Joe's gut churned. He knew Cooper meant what he said, but he could neither fathom nor accept it. "You're just being a stubborn old fool, aren't you? I mean, why not hear me out before you—"

"You're absolutely right!" Cooper snapped, his chin quivering with anger. "I'm old and I'm stubborn, but I'm not a fool. I haven't taken on an assignment in over twenty years, and I'm not taking one on now!"

"No, you're not a fool, Dylan. You're an, an—an—" Joe paused, searching for something vicious. "An ungrateful fool!"

"Ungrateful, eh?! I wouldn't worry about making money if I

were you. It's clear you've got all the makings of a successful businessman!" Cooper snarled and spit the word out like an expletive.

Every muscle in Joe's body stiffened. His hands tightened into white-knuckled fists. Cooper saw them and cocked his head in defiance. They stood there seething, eyes locked in mutual hatred and disdain, neither wanting to strike the first blow, nor be the one to weaken and back down.

The tense silence was shattered by the creak of a hinge. Alicia was standing in the doorway in absolute shock. "Joe? What happened? My God, I was just dozing off. I thought I was having a nightmare. I—"

"Stubborn old fool!"

"Joe—" Alicia admonished sharply. She reached out and took hold of Cooper's arm as he charged past her. "Dylan, please?"

Cooper thundered across the parlor without breaking stride, then paused in front of the Christmas tree, his eyes welling with remorse. "I'm sorry, Alicia." He hurried from the bungalow, slamming the door after him. Alicia jumped at the sharp report, then stood there in stunned silence.

"Stubborn fool!" Joe bellowed, shaking with rage. He swept the copy of Cooper's book from the table. It hit the floor with a loud thump and went sliding into a pot of poinsettias in the corner.

"What happened?" Alicia asked again. "I mean . . . it's . . . it's Christmas Eve. I . . . I just can't believe you . . . you and Dylan . . . fighting like enemies. Why?"

Joe shrugged sullenly and turned away.

"This is supposed to be a time of happiness and joy," she said, trembling with emotion. "Joe?"

Joe ignored her and stared out the window in silence for a moment. "You know that old saying, the best laid plans of mice and men? Well, you can add God to that list."

Cooper was coming down the steps from the porch when he felt his chest tighten, and began wheezing audibly. He leaned against the truck for a moment, his breath coming in thin gray puffs; then he struggled into the cab and drove off into the blinding snow that came at an angle from the sea.

PART THREE

To save us all from Satan's power,
When we were gone astray . . .

PART THREE

Chapter Nineteen

Several days had passed. Alicia was tidying up the kitchen after breakfast when Joe came through the door from the garage carrying some boxes.

"Where are you going with those?"

"Inside," he replied, evading the question.

Alicia hurried after him into the parlor. "Why? What are you doing?"

"I'm taking down the tree."

"The Christmas tree? It isn't even New Year's yet. We always leave it up until the sixth."

"Not this year," Joe said with finality, setting the boxes on the coffee table. "Look at it. The branches are drooping. The needles are all dry . . ."

"Well, it probably just needs some water."

"Too late for that now," Joe declared, removing one of the ornaments. "It's on its last legs. I'm getting rid of it."

Alicia stepped in front of the tree protectively. "You don't stand a chance and you know it."

"It's dangerous," Joe persisted, about to remove another ornament. "It could catch fire. It's outlived its usefulness and it's got to go."

Alicia stood her ground and locked her eyes with his, stopping him; then her expression softened and she broke into a knowing smile. "I wasn't sure what this was all about, at first, but I think I know now."

"You do?"

"Uh-huh," she replied smugly. "What could possibly have caused you to come charging in here this morning and declare that our Christmas tree has, and I quote, 'outlived its usefulness'?"

Joe shrugged. "I'm not sure I follow you."

"I'm not surprised."

"I hate when you do this, Alicia. Come on, what are you talking about?"

"Your disagreement with Dylan."

"Oh. What about it?"

"Peace on earth. Good will toward men, Joe. I think it's time you got back into the Christmas spirit, and got over it. You owe him an apology."

"You don't stand a chance and you know it," Joe retorted, purposely repeating her earlier response.

"Oh, Joe," Alicia sighed. "He's lived an entire lifetime according to his code. Do you really expect him to change now?"

"Yes, I do," Joe replied with an exasperated groan. "He's so . . . so . . . stubborn."

"Especially when he's right."

"When he's right?!" Joe erupted.

"He is, Joe. You're just too proud to admit it. Your father's sweat gave you this business; and Dylan's book saved it for you; but now you're going to have to—"

"Dylan's book?!" Joe interrupted angrily. "It's yours, and mine, and Gundy's, and Lucas's too. It's the least Dylan could do to show his appreciation!"

Alicia took a deep breath, reconsidering. "You're right to

care about your employees, Joe," she conceded, softening her tone. "But you're wrong about Dylan; and if you're honest with yourself, you'll start the New Year off right and resolve to make it the rest of the way on your own."

Joe held her look in angry silence, then his eyes flickered with a thought. "I just might do that," he said in a spiteful tone. He scooped up the boxes and charged back through the kitchen and into the garage.

Alicia fetched the ornament Joe had removed from the tree and hung it on a branch; then noticed that one of the figures in the creche had toppled. She stooped and righted it, and was repositioning the others around the manger just so, when she heard the roadster start up.

Joe drove straight to the printing shop, called Lucas Bartlett, and told him he had a job he might find interesting. A half hour later, the young photographer was in Joe's office listening to his proposal.

"That's very interesting," Bartlett said, mulling it over. The fire in the potbellied stove had long ago died, and they sat bundled in hats, coats and gloves. "A project like that could keep us all busy for years."

"That's the idea. You think you're up to it?"

"You bet I am," Bartlett replied with a cocky grin. "Still something I don't get, though. Why isn't Cooper taking the pictures?"

"Because he's a stubborn old fool. You know how set in his ways he can be."

Bartlett's eyes rolled. "I wouldn't work with him again if it was the last job on earth."

Joe smiled sagely. "Well, sometimes these things have a way of paying off in the end. I imagine you're more than familiar with any special techniques he uses."

"Special techniques?" Bartlett echoed with a derisive sneer. "Archaic'd be more like it. Chemicals, paper, a bare light bulb. That's it, that's all he—" Bartlett paused as it dawned on him. "Oh, oh, I get it. You want me to copy his style . . ."

"I wouldn't blame you for being offended, Lucas," Joe offered. "But I didn't think it'd be fair for me to make the decision for you."

The young photographer considered it for a moment, then cocked his head challengingly. "Whose name is going to be on the books? Cooper's or mine?"

"Yours, of course."

"Then there's nothing to be offended about," Bartlett said.

"Good. Put together some samples as fast as you can," Joe instructed, shaking Bartlett's hand. He waited until Bartlett had left the office then pulled off a glove and lifted the phone. His finger spun the dial, once, twice, then paused with uncertainty. He hung up, wrestling with what he was about to do. The silence reminded him of how close the shop had come to being silent forever, of how desperate he felt at the prospect of failure, of how his employees had come through for him and had every right to expect him to do the same for them.

Joe dialed again. Resolutely, this time. "Arthur? Joe Clements calling. I'm not in the habit of doing business over the holidays, but I've got some good news."

Arthur Hastings sat next to a window in the study of his elegantly furnished home. Beyond the frosty panes that framed a Christmas tree, the Charles River cut a graceful swath through Back Bay Boston. "You've talked to Cooper about the assignment," he declared, setting his newspaper aside.

"Yes. Yes, I did," Joe said, trying to keep any hint of disappointment from his voice. "To make a long story short, we're ready to go to work whenever you are."

"Good. Let's meet in my office, on Monday. Say about eleven?"

"Monday, at eleven it is."

"Looking forward to it," Hastings concluded brightly. "After all I've heard about Cooper, I'm quite anxious to meet him."

Chapter Twenty

Cooper's truck was parked in front of Dr. Cheever's stately house that was blanketed with snow. The front door opened, and the old fellow came onto the porch pulling on a sheepskin parka as he trudged to the pickup. Chronic consumption was the diagnosis. A ban on pipe-smoking and less time spent in his fume-filled darkroom, the remedy.

The engine coughed and sputtered, refusing to start, when Cooper turned the key. It sounded like the old truck's death rattle, he thought. He jammmed his pipe into the corner of his mouth and gave it one last try. It finally kicked over, chugging erratically as he drove off. The weary truck was snaking along shoreline road when the engine started sputtering again. Cooper thumbed the lever on the steering column, advancing the spark, but the engine gasped and wheezed and finally died.

Cooper groaned in disgust and guided the truck onto the shoulder. He took a moment to gather his strength, then got out and hinged up the bonnet. All the ignition wires appeared fastened, but he fetched a wrench and began tightening them anyway. He was still at it when he heard a vehicle approaching and came out from under the bonnet in search of help. The sight of Joe's roadster sent him ducking back into the engine compartment with a scowl.

Joe's mind was on the dilemma Hastings had just unknowingly created for him, and he hadn't noticed the disabled vehicle from afar; but, as he neared and slowed to offer his assistance, his eyes widened in angry recognition. Serves the old fool right, Joe thought as he stepped on the gas.

Cooper spat on the ground as the roadster roared past, then got back into the truck. It took several attempts but the balky engine finally caught. Cooper let it idle, got out again, and closed the bonnet with an angry slam. Old friends may be the best kind, he thought, but this one was letting him down. He stood, hands on hips, glaring at the beat up old truck, then his eyes softened with empathy. "Guess we're both about ready for the scrap heap."

Chapter Twenty-One

Alicia was in the parlor hanging several prints of Cooper's Christmas pictures next to the one of the bungalow when the phone rang. She cleaned her hands on her apron and answered it. "Mr. Hastings, how are you? Just fine, thanks—No, he isn't. Have you tried the shop?—Oh, then he's probably on his way. I'll have him call you soon as he gets home—Oh, sure, good idea. I'd be happy to." She nodded as she jotted on a pad, then her jaw slackened and her eyes narrowed with concern at the content of Hastings's message. A short time later, she heard the roadster pulling into the drive.

Joe took the steps to the porch two at a time, and sauntered into the parlor where Alicia was waiting. "Hi," he said, sensing her mood. "What's up?"

"Arthur Hastings just called."

Joe's stomach fluttered with apprehension. "Hastings?" he echoed, doing his best to conceal it.

"Yes. He said he forgot he has an appointment on Monday morning and wants to meet at two instead. He said to call back if it was a problem."

Joe shrugged, trying to appear nonchalant. There was something about Alicia now, something condemning or judgmental in the way she held herself, that unsettled him. "No, two o'clock's all right."

Alicia studied him out of the corner of her eye. "You didn't say anything about a meeting."

"Well, you said to find a way to make it on my own, and that's what I'm doing."

"Yes, I'm afraid so."

"What do you mean by that?"

"Well, Mr. Hastings just happened to mention how pleased he was that you were able to convince Dylan to take on the assignment."

"Why wouldn't he be?" Joe challenged, in a bold lie. He held her look for a moment, then sent a threatening glance to the Christmas tree. "I still say it should go."

"And we say it shouldn't," Alicia retorted firmly.

"—And those along with it," Joe added, having noticed the Christmas pictures she'd hung.

"Sorry, majority rules," she declared, cradling her tummy. "You were just out-voted two to one."

On Monday morning, the Christmas tree and Cooper's pictures still graced the parlor; Alicia was still troubled; and Joe was on the train to Boston.

Hastings and Brown's offices were in an impressive limestone building on Hanover Street, a short walk from North Station. The smell of leather and cigars mixed with the scent of freshly cut pine from the Christmas tree in the reception area; and despite the uncertain economy, the place was alive with bustling employees and the clatter of adding machines, typewriters, and telephones.

Hastings looked puzzled as he shook Joe's hand. "Where's Cooper? I expected he'd be with you?"

"So did I," Joe replied unflinchingly. He knew Hastings would ask, and had spent the journey deciding how he'd respond. "I did my best to convince him to come along; but you know how he is."

Hastings shrugged in resignation. "I guess we'll have to chalk it up to artistic temperament, won't we?"

"I guess so," Joe said, forcing a smile. "I'll just have to continue acting as an intermediary."

"I don't see that we have a choice."

Joe nodded, relieved to be past it. "Let's talk about subject matter, Arthur."

"Fine. Where do you want to begin?"

"With people. The first volume should be about people. I want it to pay tribute to their spirit; to their determination to survive; to their belief that this is still the land of opportunity. I want to see it in their faces, in their eyes, in their hands"—He paused, then, in a voice that rang with emotion, concluded—"in their souls."

Hastings was moved by Joe's fervor and took a moment to reply. "That's an excellent choice, Joe. It's all up to Cooper now."

"It certainly is." Joe sensed that a chance to prepare him for the inevitable moment of truth was at hand, and casually added, "Up to a point, anyway."

Hastings's brows arched. "I'm not sure I follow you?"

"Well, it dawned on me that no matter who takes them, it still comes down to the pictures in the end."

Hastings cocked his head thoughtfully. "True. I can't argue with that."

Joe suppressed a sigh of relief and nodded.

Chapter Twenty-Two

The roadster wound along the snow-packed road to Cooper's house, and parked next to the faded pickup.

Alicia hurried from the car, carrying a worn mackinaw. "Dylan?" she called out, knocking on the door. "Dylan, it's Alicia." She brightened at the sound of footsteps and the creak of hinges that followed.

"Oh, I was hoping you'd come to see me," Cooper exclaimed with delight as they lunged into each other's arms. "Come on in. I'll put up some water for tea."

"I'd love to, but dinner's on the stove. I can't stay." She held up the mackinaw. "You left this at our place. I just wanted to drop it off and say hello."

"Thank you. We've been together a long time. Now, I have something for you—so to speak."

Alicia turned up her collar against the cold and waited in the entry as Cooper hurried off and returned with a small teddy bear.

Alicia's eyes widened like a child's. "Oh, Dylan you didn't have to do that."

"Of course I did," Cooper enthused, pleased to be sharing a moment of happiness with her. "I'd planned on waiting until the blessed event, but thought it best to take advantage of the moment."

Alicia hugged the stuffed animal to her bosom, then, prompted by her conversation with Hastings and by Joe's troubling reaction, she added, "I can't wait to show it to Joe."

Cooper bristled at the name, but maintained his composure. "Well," he said in a formal tone that was uncharacteristic, "He's yours now, Alicia. You're free to do with him what you will."

Alicia's shoulders sagged in disappointment, not at Cooper's words, but at his detached tone which confirmed her suspicions. "I take it you and Joe—you haven't talked, have you?"

Dylan shook his head no emphatically. "Not since we— well—since I saw you last," he replied, shaken by the memory. "Why do you ask?"

Alicia shrugged, deciding against confiding in him until she'd given Joe a chance to explain. "Just wishful thinking, I guess."

"I'm afraid I can't make that wish come true."

"I know," Alicia whispered, her eyes glistening with emotion.

"Now, now, none of that," the old fellow scolded. "Promise me you'll come by again soon?"

Alicia wiped away a tear, and nodded.

Cooper was hugging her when Alicia kissed his cheek, then hurried to the car. He watched her drive off as he had the last time, remaining in the doorway long after she was gone. Once again, a surge of emotion set his mind racing through decades past; and once again, the memories were just as strong, the sense of loss just as painful, and the chance of ever seeing his beloved Grace again, just as hopeless.

Chapter Twenty-Three

Moonlight painted the bungalow with a bluish glow that spilled through the window into the kitchen where Alicia was clearing dishes. Joe was sitting at the table with a cup of coffee. The meeting with Hastings had improved his disposition, but he'd kept a smug silence about it.

"Joe," Alicia finally said, breaking it. "Joe, we have to talk about something. I was going to mention it before but I didn't want to spoil dinner."

"So you decided to spoil the rest of the evening instead . . ." he said, sounding facetious.

"I went to see Dylan this morning."

Joe's eyes sharpened to pinpoints. "You what?"

"You heard me. I went to see Dylan."

"That's a heck of a way to start the New Year." He got to his feet, glaring at her with anger and disbelief. "Whose side are you on anyway?"

"It's not about taking sides, Joe. It's about truthfulness. I didn't want to say anything until I was sure. Dylan isn't taking the pictures, is he?"

"I never said he was."

"Maybe, *you* didn't say it, but Mr. Hastings did," Alicia retorted, on the verge of losing her temper. "If Dylan isn't taking them, who is?"

"Lucas," Joe replied.

"I see . . . But Mr. Hastings doesn't know that, does he?" she challenged, her eyes burning with condemnation. "It's not like you to be deceptive, Joe."

"I'm not being deceptive, Alicia. I'm being smart. I knew it'd be impossible to convince Hastings to use another photographer, so I decided to show him instead."

"Show him?"

"Yes. You know what they say: A picture's worth a thousand words? Well, once he sees the pictures, sees how good they are, he won't care who took them."

"Okay," she said crossing her arms. "Then what?"

"Then," Joe repeated, pausing before delivering the punch line, "then I'll tell Hastings the truth."

Alicia's face fell. Her posture slackened. She was stopped cold. "Oh."

"Right. Oh," Joe said, implying he'd been vindicated. "Hastings has to meet a payroll every week just like me. Given an equal alternative, he's not going to let a cantankerous old man stand in the way."

"I guess not," Alicia conceded, feeling she'd judged him rashly. "Looks like I owe you an apology."

Joe smirked.

"Don't gloat. It's not becoming."

"I'm waiting, Alicia."

"I apologize."

"Thank you." Joe punctuated it with a snap of his head, then pushed past her and left the kitchen.

Alicia gathered her thoughts, then found Joe at the rolltop desk in the parlor, sorting through papers. She fetched the teddy bear Cooper had given her from amongst the gifts under the Christmas tree, and set it on the desk in front of Joe. "Isn't he cute?"

"Sure is," Joe replied, his mood brightening. "Where'd he come from?"

"Dylan gave him to me," Alicia replied a little too brightly. "I thought you'd like to see it."

Joe's expression darkened. He grasped one of the teddy's floppy ears between thumb and forefinger, as if the stuffed animal was contaminated, and handed it back to her. "Okay. I've seen it." Joe swiveled around in the chair, and resumed sorting papers as if she wasn't there.

Chapter Twenty-Four

The temperature had dropped into the teens, and the pot-bellied stove was creaking in protest as Bartlett covered the layout table in Joe's office with his sample photographs: proud faces and gnarled hands; blue-collar workers and hardscrabble farm families; bright-eyed children and blissful infants. "I think I've got the old guy's style down pretty good."

Joe nodded smartly in agreement. "I'd say so. I can't wait to show them to Hastings."

The next afternoon, despite a snowstorm that wrought havoc with the train schedule, Joe was in Boston spreading the photographs across the table in Hastings and Brown's conference room.

Hastings circled the table, studying each picture. "I don't know, Joe," he finally said with grave expression. "There's something missing."

Joe's stomach began tighting into a knot. "Missing? What do you mean?"

"Well, they have the technical polish I expected. But they fall short artistically. They're just not up to Cooper's standards. They're stiff and awkward. Like—like pictures of machines."

Joe looked stunned. "Machines? Gosh, Arthur, I—I thought they were pretty good."

"They are," Hastings said with an enigmatic pause. "Just not good enough. Cooper always said he wasn't interested in taking on assignments. Now we know why."

"I guess," Joe said, his mind racing to find a way to salvage the project. "I'm sure if I told him what you said, he could make some adjustments and—"

"You'd be wasting your time, Joe. Some people, no matter how talented, can't channel their creativity to someone else's vision. We were wrong to force him."

Joe emitted a forlorn sigh, realizing that neither pressing the lie nor telling the truth would affect Hastings's decision.

"You know," Hastings went on, holding one of the prints to the light. "If I didn't know better, I'd think someone was trying to copy Cooper's style."

Joe swallowed hard, then looked Hastings square in the eye. "You're right, Arthur. Someone was. You probably won't believe this, but I was planning to tell you. I just wanted you to see them first." Joe lowered his eyes and went about collecting the prints.

Hastings watched with growing empathy. Every business had its ups and downs. He'd experienced Joe's desperation more times than he cared to remember; and, despite the sleight of hand, he admired the young man's tenacity and willingness to take chances to keep his business from failing. "You know, I feel badly about this, Joe," he finally said.

Joe shrugged in resignation. "So do I."

Hastings looked off thoughtfully for a moment. "Come to think of it, there's a project in the offing. No guarantees, but I may be able to steer it your way."

Joe nodded weakly in acknowledgment.

"Nothing like this of course; but it's right up your alley: a catalogue . . . mail order stuff. I should have word in a few days."

"That'd be swell, Arthur," Joe said. He forced a smile, and placed the last photographs into the leather folio.

"By the way, I recall you mentioning a photographer you've used for this kind of work. What was his name again? Barton? Bennett?"

"Bartlett," Joe replied in a barely audible voice. "Lucas Bartlett."

"That's it. Think he might be available?"

"Yes," Joe muttered, stung by the irony. "I have a feeling he might."

A short while later on the train back to Newbury, Joe slouched in his seat, staring out the window at the wintry land-scape racing past. Hypnotized by the fleeting images and the rhythmic clack of train wheels, he was thinking about how, after saving his company and keeping his employees from losing their jobs, he had somehow lost his way and broken his integrity to get the second book published.

He'd always been an honest man who prided himself on his word being his bond. Now he felt ashamed at his greed and un-characteristic deceptiveness, and guilt-ridden over his falling out with Cooper, not to mention how he had quarreled with Alicia and scorned her goodness and sense of decency.

It was almost dusk when the train arrived in Newbury. Joe trudged through the snow to the roadster, carrying the portfolio, then slipped behind the wheel and lit a cigarette. That morning, he had driven himself to the station to keep Alicia off the treach-erous roads. Now, as he drove the icy ribbon that paralleled the coast, the feelings of shame and guilt he'd felt on the train resur-faced with overwhelming force.

Like a wounded animal retreating to its lair, Joe wanted noth-ing more than to get home and take refuge in Alicia's reassuring embrace; but his heart was pounding like a pile driver, and his breath was coming in short tight puffs, and his brow was dotted with perspiration despite the cold, and he suddenly pulled off onto the shoulder, unable to cope with the unnerving torment. He dragged deeply on his cigarette, exhaling slowly as if expelling the demons that had taken hold of him, and sat there atop the bluff, staring down at the storm-tossed sea, his anxiety soaring with each metronomic sweep of the wipers across the windshield.

Chapter Twenty-Five

The same morning, the gusting winds that sent the snow-storm slashing across the harbor were threatening to blow Cooper off the ice-encrusted breakwater into the raging surf below. Gurgling torrents swirled about his scuffed hightops as he bent to his Graflex. In the distance, where the blizzard marched over snow-capped mountains, a shaft of light pierced the cloud cover, turning each flake of snow into a sparkling gemstone. Cooper made a half dozen exposures, capturing the visual tour de force in all its glory, then hurried back to his darkroom with his booty.

He spent the rest of the morning developing the negatives and was about to make his first print when the muffled ring of the phone came from the cottage. As always, he assumed it would stop after several rings, and whoever it was would call back if it was really important; but this time, the phone rang and rang. Cooper set his negative aside and went into the cottage to answer it. "Cooper."

"Dylan? Dylan, oh, thank God you're there," Alicia exclaimed, trying to catch her breath. "I'm—I'm—" she gasped, lurching back against the sofa.

"Lass? What is it, lass? Are you all right?"

"The baby," Alicia blurted in the throes of a contraction. "Doctor Cheever said it wouldn't be for a couple more weeks but—" She suddenly stiffened and gasped, cradling her tummy.

"The baby—the baby," Cooper's voice rose with excitement. "You're going to have the baby."

"Yes, yes, Joe isn't here and I've no way to get to the hospital. I called Dr. Cheever but there was no answer. Hurry, please?"

"Hold on, lass. I'm on my way."

The old fellow dashed from the cottage pulling on his mackinaw and climbed into the pickup. The engine refused to start, and he was beside himself by the time it finally kicked over. He slammed it in gear and headed down the hill, pushing the old vehicle to the limit, the worn tires slipping and sliding on the icy roads. Fifteen minutes later, he turned into the drive behind the Clements's bungalow. Cooper got out and left the engine running.

"Alicia?" he called out, his anxiety soaring as he burst into the parlor. "Alicia, are you all right?"

Alicia hadn't moved from the sofa. Teeth clenched against the onset of another contraction, she responded with an affirmative nod.

"Good," Cooper grunted. "Better gather your things, lass. Hurry. No telling how long it'll take us to get to hospital with these roads."

Alicia started to rise, then stiffened again. "No. No, Dylan, it's too late. We'll never make it."

"Never make it?" Cooper echoed with disbelief. "Am I to take that to mean that—"

"Yes," Alicia interrupted. "The baby's coming, now." She emitted a painful gasp, then another, arching back against the cushions. "Right now. Better help me into bed, then try Dr. Cheever again."

Cooper took her arm and guided her down the hall toward the bedroom, his mind racing through decades past to another such night; to another young woman, his beloved Grace, frightened and alone; to the child he never knew, the infant son he had come home from the war to learn was with the Lord in Heaven. Shaken by the memories, his eyes glistening with emotion, he helped Alicia into the bed, then hurried back to the parlor and dialed the phone.

Chapter Twenty-Six

The Newbury Community Church was darkened at this hour except for the soft glow of a light above the altar. Pastor Martin came from a door in an alcove next to the altar and strode up the aisle, squinting to identify the figure hunched in the last pew. "Joe?" he wondered with uncertainty as he approached. "Joe Clements?"

Joe shifted anxiously and nodded.

"I thought I heard a car," the pastor explained, then in an attempt at levity, added, "I'll do anything to avoid facing paperwork. Even minister to a congregant."

Joe smiled thinly. "But you didn't expect it would be me. Did you, Pastor Martin?"

"No, I can't say I did; but it's good to see you, Joseph. I recall encouraging Alicia to bring you to Sunday services."

"This couldn't wait until Sunday, Pastor Martin."

"That sounds serious," the pastor said, slipping into the pew next to him. "How can I help you?"

Joe shrugged with pained uncertainty. "I'm not sure you can. I'm not sure anyone can. I'm not even sure why I'm here. Really. All I know is, we had a wonderful Christmas, and then everything started going wrong. I feel like my whole world's falling apart. This meeting I had today was the last straw." He shook his head and groaned in despair. "I just wanted to get home to Alicia; but all of a sudden I felt so . . . so . . . overwhelmed . . .

that I had to pull over. I just couldn't go home like this. I . . . I guess, with the baby coming, I was afraid of upsetting her. I was trying to sort things out when I thought of something she said on the way home from the Christmas play and . . . and here I am."

"Well, I'm glad you are," Pastor Martin said softly. "Now let's talk about what's troubling you."

Joe splayed his hands in a helpless gesture. "I don't know, I'm . . . I'm just not myself . . . I feel confused and cornered." He shifted in the pew and folded his arms as if trying to contain himself, then unfolded them and began tugging at his shirt collar. "Truth is, I feel so guilty. My father taught me to be a man of integrity . . . to always tell the truth and keep my word."

Pastor Martin nodded with empathy. "Guilt is common to all human beings, Joe. God gave each of us a conscience, and when we violate it, we feel bad. I'm sure you can think of a good reason for your guilt."

"A half dozen of 'em," Joe blurted, launching into a litany of his offenses that poured out of him like water bursting from a dam. "I've been selfish and prideful and . . . and . . . yes, deceitful. I'm guilty of being greedy and unreasonable, too. Not to mention disrespectful to my wife and . . . and downright mean-spirited to the person most responsible for keeping my business from going under." The deluge ended only after his falling out with Cooper and his attempt to deceive Hastings had been spelled out in detail.

"Well," Pastor Martin sighed as if trying to catch his breath. "It sounds as if you've given the Seven Deadly Sins quite a run for their money . . ." He paused and smiled at what he was about to say. ". . . Though I don't recall any mention of gluttony or sloth."

"I'm sure it wasn't for lack of trying."

"Yes, I do recall, you're not the sort to do things half way, are you?"

Joe managed a smile but it was the truth of the pastor's re-mark, not its humor, that hit home. "No, now that you mention it, Pastor Martin, I'm not; and that's the worst part. I've always been able to . . . to handle things on my own. If I have a prob-lem, I tackle it head on; and I keep at it till it's solved. I've never been in this situation before . . . never felt the need to ask for anyone's help . . . let alone God's." His shoulders sagged under the weight of his own observation, and he sighed, seeming to-tally dispirited. "I guess, I better add hypocritical to that list, too, shouldn't I?"

"Well, I think we've had quite enough mea culpas for one day," the pastor said, unmoved by Joe's self-pity; then his ex-pression softened. "You know, many of us instinctively tend to draw closer to our Creator when beset by adversity. I think that's probably one of the reasons He allows it. The more we feel as if we're not in control of events, the more we're prone to acknowl-edge the existence of a God who is in control. With every day, the world is becoming a more chaotic place, a more . . . formida-ble adversary. It's not only difficult, but foolish to try to cope with it alone."

Joe responded with a sheepish nod. "That's exactly what Alicia's been trying to tell me, but I wouldn't listen to her. Instead, when things went wrong I tried to convince her—along with myself, of course—that I had a perfectly good reason for doing what I did; but . . . but . . . the end doesn't justify the means, does it?"

"No," Pastor Martin replied. "But of course we think it's much easier to dismiss an ethical lapse if it's born of a well-in-tentioned effort."

Joe nodded. "It sure is; but it's not working, Pastor Martin. Not working at all. As I said, I'm not myself. It's . . . it's as if I've become someone I don't recognize. Someone . . . someone who I . . ." He bit off the sentence as the source of his unbearable turmoil dawned on him; then his eyes hardened and, in a condemning tone, he concluded, ". . . someone who I don't like."

Pastor Martin nodded with the wisdom of his experience. "You're a decent soul at heart, Joe. It's not surprising that, try as you might to justify your behavior as being a benefit to others, your conscience isn't buying it. Instead of giving you peace with God, it's making you feel guilty before God. And peace of mind is something you want, especially during Christmas. That's really it, isn't it?"

Joe sighed with relief and nodded.

"Well, the mere fact that you're here is powerful evidence that you know what you have to do next."

Joe nodded, again, resolutely; and enumerated in reply: "Swallow my pride, confess my sins before God, apologize to the people I've hurt, and—most important of all—find a way to make things right with Cooper."

"Sounds like a sensible course of action," Pastor Martin said, his eyes brightening at the mention of Cooper's name. "Extraordinarily talented fellow. That was quite a lovely book you published, wasn't it?"

"You've seen it?"

"Of course, who hasn't? I've a copy in my office. Even bought several as Christmas gifts. Lovely picture of the church, by the way. Did you know he got married here?"

Joe looked surprised. "Cooper?"

Pastor Martin nodded. "Almost twenty years ago. I performed the ceremony."

Joe's eyes widened with intrigue. "So . . . so you knew his wife? You knew Grace?"

Pastor's Martin's eyes clouded with sadness. "A lovely young woman. Intelligent, spirited, much like Alicia in many ways. Theirs is a tragic story."

"Yes, I know," Joe said, his voice reduced to a contrite whisper. "I guess I should be counting my blessings, shouldn't I?"

"Indeed, and as I understand it, you've had your share as of late, not to mention another on the way. You know, in my experience, making peace with God is the first step to making peace with oneself and with those we're estranged from. We all tend to lose our way at some time or other . . ." Pastor Martin paused, then glanced to the cross that hung above the altar. "Always remember, Joe—He didn't die on that cross for people who are perfect, but for sinners like you and me. And there is no sin in the world that He cannot forgive if we ask Him. The shining example is the thief who was crucified alongside of Jesus. When he asked for forgiveness, Jesus promised him that '. . . on this day you will be with me in paradise.' By inviting Him into your heart and asking Him for forgiveness, He can, as the Bible says, 'make you white as snow'."

"Thanks, Pastor Martin. Thanks for everything," Joe said, extending a hand. "Oh, and Happy New Year."

"Yes, Happy New Year, Joe," Pastor Martin said, pleased he had helped Joe put things right. He patted him on the shoulder, then slipped out of the pew and melted into the shadows of the darkened church.

Joe sat there for a moment in quiet reflection, then fell to his knees, bowed his head in prayer, confessed his sins, and invited Christ into his life.

Chapter Twenty-Seven

Darkness had fallen by the time Joe arrived at the bungalow. The roadster's headlights swept across two vehicles parked in the drive. One was Cooper's pickup; the other, a black sedan that Joe recognized as Dr. Cheever's Packard. He bolted from the car and dashed inside, his heart pounding so hard he could hear it.

Joe burst into the parlor to find Dr. Cheever sitting on the sofa sipping a brandy, and Cooper in one of the wicker chairs, calmly smoking his pipe. The old fellow stiffened at the sight of him, glaring in condemnation. Joe was too upset to notice and exclaimed, "What happened? Is everything okay?"

"Yes, mother and son are doing just fine," Cheever replied getting to his feet to shake Joe's hand. "Congratulations."

"Mother and son?!" Joe echoed in amazement. "You're sure? You're positive?" he went on rapid fire. "They're both all right?"

Cheever responded with an emphatic nod.

"But—but I thought it wasn't going to be for a couple more weeks?"

"So did I," Cheever replied, his eyes smiling from behind rimless glasses. "Evidently, your boy has a mind of his own. Would you like to see him?"

"Oh. Oh, yes," Joe replied, still stunned by the turn of events. "Of course I would."

Cooper remained behind as Cheever led the way into the bedroom. All the pillows were propped against the headboard, and Alicia was sitting up, nursing the baby. "Hi, darling," she whispered.

"Gosh, I'm—I'm so sorry," Joe sighed, riddled with guilt. "I'd have never gone, if I'd known . . ."

"Oh, Joe, how could you have known?" Alicia said, absolving him. "Dr. Cheever says he's a little trouper. Ten fingers, ten toes, an appetite like his father's . . . Want to hold him?"

Joe hesitated for a moment, then took the baby and cradled him in his arms, awkwardly; but the tiny, peaceful face peering from within the blanket seemed to soothe his uneasiness. "He's beautiful, darling," Joe whispered with the combined sense of excitement, pride and awe that touches every new parent. "I don't know how to thank you, Doc," he said, turning to Cheever. "But, I promise you, I'll find a way."

"Me?" Cheever wondered. "I was making a house call down in Rowley. It was all over by the time I got here. Don't thank me, thank Dylan. God knows what might have happened if it wasn't for him."

Joe let out a long breath and glanced at Alicia. No words were necessary. He had sorted it out with Pastor Martin and had made his peace with God, and his eyes said it all.

Alicia sensed the profound change in him and shifted her gaze to the door.

Joe knew exactly what she was thinking and nodded. "I'll be right back." He nestled the baby in Alicia's arms, and went into the parlor to make his peace with Cooper, but the old fellow was gone.

Joe heard the truck sputtering and refusing to start, and hurried to the door. Just as he opened it, the engine kicked over and Cooper slammed the truck in gear. Joe was on the verge of calling out and running after him, but despite his need to make amends, Joe suddenly sensed his apology should be something special, something that went beyond words, and remained in the doorway as the truck went down the drive.

The next morning, awakened early by the baby's hungry cry, Joe headed into the kitchen and made some breakfast. He was carrying a tray laden with toast, coffee, butter, and jam to the bedroom when he glanced into the parlor and was surprised to see Alicia standing in front of the Christmas tree with the baby.

"Alicia?" Joe said with concern. "Didn't Dr. Cheever say you were supposed to stay in bed?"

"He certainly did," she replied with a mischievous twinkle. "But I don't think he'd disapprove of me showing Joseph Clements Jr. his first Christmas tree."

"Oh," Joe said, a little chagrined; then in a self-deprecating tone, joked, "See? Aren't you glad I talked you out of taking it down?"

Alicia laughed and settled on the sofa with the baby. Joe sat next to her and began stirring his coffee, lost in his thoughts.

Alicia sensed what was troubling him, and took his hand in hers. "It didn't go very well with Mr. Hastings yesterday, did it?"

"No, I'm afraid not," Joe replied with a defeated sigh. "I guess I never appreciated just how special Dylan's talent is."

"How special he is, Joe."

Joe nodded in contrite agreement. "I was the one who was being stubborn and foolish."

"Not to mention greedy, selfish, and downright ornery," Alicia teased.

"I know. I'm sorry. I've said hurtful things and—"

"Shush," she whispered, putting a finger to his lips to silence him.

"Okay, but I thought you'd be pleased to know it was Pastor Martin who helped me sort things out."

"Pastor Martin?"

"See? I knew that'd get your attention. I stopped by to see him on the way home yesterday. That's why I was late."

"Oh, Joe . . ."

"You know, you were right. For the first time in my life, I have real peace with God."

Alicia's eyes glistened with emotion. "This is the best Christmas gift of all, Joe."

Joe smiled, savoring the moment, then glancing down to the baby, said, "I think we should call it a tie."

"So do I," Alicia replied in a way that suggested she was up to something. "Now, I don't mean to sound selfish or anything, but there is one more gift that I'm still praying for."

"I'm working on it," Joe said with an impish smile, knowing she was referring to his making peace with Cooper.

Alicia looked puzzled. "Working on it? Repeat after me: I'm sorry, Dylan. I was wrong. I apologize. I hope you'll forgive me. It's that simple, isn't it?"

"Yes, but I want to give him something too; something special to make sure he knows I really mean it. I want him to know how badly I feel and how much I value his friendship." Joe fetched the teddy bear from beneath the tree and tucked it next to his newborn son. He was thinking about what that gift might be when he noticed the Christmas pictures that Alicia had hung next to the one of the bungalow. One of them—the picture of Grace walking in the wintery landscape—held Joe's attention for a long moment, then his eyes came to life with the special idea he sought.

That afternoon when Alicia and the baby were napping, Joe made sure the bedroom door was closed, then went to his desk and called Hastings at his office in Boston. Joe told him he was working on a special project, a very special and personal one that involved Cooper, and asked for his help.

Chapter Twenty-Eight

Almost a month of the new year had passed. The snow had stopped. The roads had been plowed. And the morning sun rose in a clear sky, but Newbury was still caught in winter's frigid grasp.

Though Joe had gotten over the impact of his fateful meeting with Hastings, he hadn't forgotten the mail order project Hastings had mentioned at its conclusion. To Joe's relief, neither had Hastings; and this morning the canny businessman had taken the train up from Boston to discuss it. The two men were in Joe's office going over the details when the mailman knocked on the half-open door.

"Morning, Ben," Joe said, brightening.

"Mr. Clements," Ben grunted, handing him a special delivery envelope. "Sorry to interrupt, but I need your John Hancock right here."

"My pleasure," Joe said, signing the receipt.

"By the way, I hear congratulations are in order."

Joe plucked a cigar from a box on his desk and handed it to Ben. "Thanks, everyone says he looks like his mother."

"Lucky boy," Ben joked, as he hurried off.

"Well," Hastings said, gesturing to the material he'd spread across the layout table, "I'd say you've got plenty to keep you busy."

"Plenty," Joe replied. "By the way, you remember that special project we spoke about?"

"Yes, I understand my people came through with the information you were after."

"They sure did. Cabled it to my office weeks ago . . ." Joe held up the special delivery envelope. ". . . and the payoff's in here."

Later that afternoon, the sun was hanging above the horizon as Joe turned into the bungalow's snow covered drive. Alicia heard the car and came to the door to greet him. "Hi, darling! How did it go?"

"Well, we've got the job . . ."

"That's wonderful," she exclaimed, leading the way inside. "I want to hear all about it."

"Frankly, I've had my fill of business for today. It's time to get on to more important matters."

Alicia's brows arched with curiosity. "Really?"

"Uh-huh. I was about to suggest we take a ride over to Dylan's."

"Dylan's?" Alicia repeated, sounding as uncertain as she did pleased.

"Yes, I have a surprise for him."

Alicia's eyes narrowed with concern. "I hope it isn't like the last one?"

Joe smiled and slipped the special delivery envelope from his pocket. "No, it's in here."

"Well, come on. What is it?"

"A steamer ticket."

"A steamer ticket?" she exclaimed.

"Uh-huh. First class cabin, round trip to Scotland in the name of one D. Cooper."

"Oh, Joe! Let's go give it to him right now!"

"Try and stop me. There's more to it, by the way."

"There is?"

"Uh-huh. Let's get Joseph bundled up and I'll tell you on the way." A short time later, they were racing along the snow-blanketed coast, Joe at the wheel. Alicia sat next to him, cradling the baby. He turned onto the road that wound through the foothills, guiding the roadster along the unplowed switchbacks to Cooper's place.

Alicia brightened at the sight of the battered truck parked outside. "Oh, good, he's here," she said, as Joe stopped next to it. They got out and hurried to the front door. Joe knocked, then knocked again. "Dylan? Dylan, you in there?" No reply, no footsteps, not a sound. "He's probably out taking pictures."

"I don't know," Alicia said, glancing at the darkening sky. "He's usually here at this hour."

Joe stepped to a window, rubbed off some frost with his glove, and peered inside. His eyes darted to Cooper's camera standing next to the fireplace. "Well, he may be out, but he's not taking pictures."

Alicia tried the door with her free hand. It creaked open, and she walked into the parlor. The frigid air was ripe with the scent of chemicals and an aroma of pipe smoke. "Dylan? Dylan, you here?" she called out, a hint of concern creeping into her voice.

"Where the heck is he?" Joe said, following her.

Alicia shrugged. A few tense seconds passed before it dawned on her. "Oh, I know," she said, relieved. "Wait here with daddy, okay?" She handed the baby to Joe and hurried off down the corridor.

The darkroom was closed. Alicia put an ear to the door; but heard neither rustling paper, nor sloshing chemicals, nor shuffling feet. She rapped on it lightly, hesitant to interrupt Cooper's work. "Dylan?" she called out. "Dylan, you in there?" Still no response. She knocked again, harder this time, then tried the knob. The door was locked from the inside and wouldn't budge. Her anxiety soared. "Dylan?! Dylan, it's Alicia. Are you all right?!" Silence. She was beside herself, and about to fetch Joe when she heard the sound of the latch lifting. The door creaked open, inviting her into the darkness. She squinted until her eyes became accustomed to the dark and found Cooper slouched in a chair. "Dylan?" she said softly, making her way through the blackness. "Dylan, you all right?"

A long moment passed before the old fellow nodded. "Aye. I'm fine. I didn't mean to frighten you."

"Then why didn't you answer?" Alicia asked, glancing about. "What are you doing in here? It doesn't look like you're work-ing."

"I'm not. I was watering the plants when I heard the car, and went to the window. When I saw you and—and—" The name caught in his throat, and he started over. "When I saw who was with you, I decided I wasn't up to having visitors."

"He knows he was wrong, Dylan."

"I recall mentioning that to him several times."

"He feels terrible. He—"

"That he should."

"Please? He wants to apologize."

"It's too late for that."

"It's never too late. He has something for you. Something special."

Cooper glowered defiantly and shook his head no. "My mind's made up on the matter."

Alicia's mind raced in search of a way to change the situation, and came up with an idea. "I thought we were friends?" she began, hoping the vulnerable timbre in her voice would reach him.

"Of course, we are," Cooper replied. "You and I, that is," he added, making the distinction.

"Old friends?" she prompted, shrewdly.

Cooper's head cocked with suspicion, then his eyes narrowed with understanding, and he nodded.

"Dependable, loyal, you can count on them and they can

count on you?" she went on rapid fire, sensing she had him where she wanted him.

The old fellow nodded again. "Aye."

"Well, I'm counting on you, Dylan."

Cooper considered it for a long moment. He jammed his unlit pipe in the corner of his mouth, conceding the point, then followed Alicia to the parlor where Joe waited with the baby. She took him from his father's arms, and drifted aside, leaving the two men staring at each other in tense silence.

"I'm sorry, Dylan," Joe finally said. "I was wrong, and I'd like to make it up to you if I can." He took the envelope from his jacket and offered it to Cooper.

The old fellow stared at it suspiciously, then sensed Alicia's eyes, and snatched it from Joe's hand, stuffing it into a pocket. "Accepted," he growled.

"No. No, you have to open it," Alicia prompted.

Cooper stiffened with resistance.

"I'm counting on you, remember?"

Cooper groaned, then retrieved the envelope and tore it open. His eyes widened at the sight of the steamer ticket that moved him beyond words.

"Well," Alicia said, beaming. "Aren't you going to say something?"

"A ticket to Scotland?" Cooper responded in an amazed whisper.

Joe sighed with relief. "Well, after all you said about wanting to get back home again, I didn't think it'd be fair to keep Grace waiting forever."

Cooper's eyes flickered with delight. "Grace? My Grace?"

"Unless you know another woman named Grace?"

"Oh Joseph. I don't know what to say." Cooper was giving his enthusiasm full rein when his eyes suddenly clouded with concern.

"What is it?" Alicia asked.

"Well it just dawned on me that if I couldn't find Grace then, it'd be next to impossible now."

Alicia and Joe exchanged knowing smiles.

"And what does that mean?" Cooper prompted.

"Oh, just a feeling," Joe replied. "But if I were a betting man, I'd wager you'll have much better luck this time."

Cooper stared at him, afraid to commit his heart to it. "You've—you've found her?"

"Well, I had a hand in it," Joe replied with a modest smile. "Remember that fellow, Hastings?"

Cooper responded with a cautious nod.

"Turns out he has a number of European suppliers. One of them is a company in Glasgow. It seems they have a few government . . . connections. So, he sent them a cable, and they got in touch with someone in the Main Social Services Office in Edinburgh, and there she was."

"And there she was, where?" Cooper wondered, bristling with curiosity.

"In a town called Stirling. She's been teaching dance in a private school there for almost twenty years. She lives in the faculty residence hall."

Cooper's eyes widened with surprise. "No wonder I couldn't find her."

"To make a long story short, arrangements are being made for her to be there in Glasgow when the steamer docks. All you have to do is book passage and drop her a note with the arrival date."

Cooper was overcome with emotion. "So many years," he said, repeating it over and over. "Why, I'd probably walk right past her."

"Perhaps, but something tells me she'll have no trouble recognizing you."

"Oh, I don't know, Joseph. I'm afraid I've changed just a wee bit too."

"I still think she'll manage somehow." Joe took something from a pocket and handed it to him. It was a snapshot of Cooper Joe had taken at the Christmas party with the box camera. Its serrated edges seemed perfectly suited to Cooper's jut-jawed defiance. "We've already sent her one of these."

Cooper chuckled at what he was about to say. "Then I've little hope she'll show up."

"Dylan," Alicia gently admonished.

The baby gurgled and seemed to be reaching for Cooper's face with his fingers.

"See? Even little Joseph agrees."

"I think it's an excellent likeness," Joe said.

Cooper studied the snapshot, then looked up misty eyed. "Aye," he conceded, his voice breaking with emotion. "It's a fine picture, Joe."

God rest ye merry gentlemen,
Let nothing you dismay . . .
Remember Christ our Savior,
Was born on Christmas Day . . .
To save us all from Satan's power,
When we were gone astray . . .
O tidings of comfort and joy,
Comfort and joy.
O tidings of comfort and joy!

Old English Song, sometimes called England's Carol
Sixteenth Century, Anonymous

We hope you didn't miss the first part
of Dylan and Grace's story.
If you did, here is an excerpt from
COME SPRING,
available now.

A brisk wind that carried a hint of spring and the fresh scent of brine was coming off the water. An armada of fishing boats returning to port extended to the horizon in a sweeping arc. Cooper and Grace walked arm in arm along the rows of slips where the vessels were docking with the day's catch.

"Lest you think I came all this way just to see if you were in the doldrums," Grace said coyly. "I've another reason as well."

Cooper gestured to some bushels of shellfish that were spilling over onto the dock. "You wouldn't have come in search of cockles and mussels, alive, alive-o, now, would you?"

"Not a bad idea now that you mention it; but I came for those," Grace replied, pointing to the box of photographs he was carrying. "Latour and his fools may not want them but I do."

"And I'd like nothing better than for you to have them, Grace," Cooper said, sounding as if there was a reason she couldn't. "But what of Colin?"

Grace looked puzzled. "Colin?"

Cooper nodded. "I did promise him I'd destroy all the prints and negatives, now, didn't I?"

"Yes, I know," Grace said with a frustrated sigh. "But they're pictures of *me*, Dylan; and I want them."

"I gave my word, Grace, and I'm in the habit of keeping it."

"Yes, and an admirable habit it is, but Colin's request was

terribly unreasonable; I see no reason why you should feel bound by it."

Cooper thought it over and nodded. "At best, they will be meager pay for all your hard work."

Grace studied him out of the corner of her eye. "You've no hope of being paid for yours, have you?"

Cooper shook his head no, his brow furrowing with concern. "What is it, lass? Are you in difficulty?"

"No. No, I'm fine," Grace replied, averting her eyes. "I was just wondering . . ."

"Aye," Cooper said with understanding. "Colin will be wondering, too. Won't he?"

Grace nodded imperceptibly.

"Well, make my apologies and tell him I'll soon be back to avoiding the landlady and begging for grace periods," Cooper said, feeling lower than he had in months. "Not to mention that I've no idea how I'll ever repay the advance I accepted from Mr. Van Dusen."

"He'll sell some of your pictures one day, Dylan. I know he will," Grace said, imploring him to believe it. "You can't lose faith in yourself."

"How could I with the likes of you around?" Cooper said, coaxing a smile out of her.

Grace stepped to the railing that ran along the water's edge and looked out across the harbor, her chin raised into the wind, her hair blowing in amber waves behind her, her long dress billowing like the mainsails of the ships at sea. The scene had an aesthetic and emotional power that raised Cooper's pores. He stood awestruck, feasting on it for a long moment; then, stepping closer, he put an arm around Grace's waist and tilted his head close to hers. "Can you stay with me for a while tonight, Grace?"

Grace turned to face him, her eyes filled with conflict. "Oh, Dylan, I want to," she replied, clearly torn by it. "But you know

Colin will be worried. Not to mention that he's expecting supper and I've yet to do my marketing."

"Aye," Cooper said forlornly. "Doubting Colin strikes again."

"Please try to understand," Grace pleaded, crushed by the disappointment in his voice. "I want to stay with you, Dylan; and truth be told I . . . I . . ." She paused, deciding whether or not she would continue. "I know I shouldn't be so forward as to say this. Lord knows it's not at all my place, but I want to stay with you forever, Dylan; and if you're of the same mind, given time, I've no doubt I shall."

"Aye, I've plenty of time, Grace, if you're saying what I think you're saying."

"Yes, I am," Grace replied in a tender whisper. "You know, my mother used to say good things come to those who wait."

The sound of a ship's bells rode the wind as Cooper gently embraced her, holding her eyes with his. "I'd wait a lifetime for you, Grace."

"And I for you," she said softly, her eyes glistening with emotion as she caressed his face with the tips of her fingers and kissed him.

And, coming this summer, the eagerly anticipated conclusion of this trilogy:

Dylan will journey across the ocean to find Grace and end their separation. His is a pilgrimage of hope, reunion, and reconciliation. But in their time apart, both he and Grace have changed, the world has changed, and it is unclear whether they can reunite and continue their lives together.